Wrong Place
Wrong Time

IKE KEEN

Paperback-Press
an imprint of A & S Publishing
A & S Holmes, Inc.

ISBN: 0692413944
ISBN-13: 978-0692413944

TABLE OF CONTENTS

ACKNOWLEDGMENTS

A heart felt thank you to Norma, who does a hell of a job editing, I couldn't do without you.

To Karen Sutherland, your input is also very important and appreciated.

To Sleuths' Ink members, thanks for all the support.

Last but not least, I'd like to thank Paperback-Press. Without Sharon I would never have perused my dream of being published.

IN THE BEGINNING

Cary Burks was my friend.

I sat across from him on the ratty old couch he slept on most of the time and smoked a cigar. He didn't deserve this. I mean, he wasn't a model citizen but he didn't deserve this. He had tried to get hold of me today; called Shelly about every ten minutes and each call she said he sounded scared. I'd been in court all day. Tomas "Little Tommy" Alto was on trial for strangling a waitress who worked at The Horned Toad, a roadhouse east of town.

Tommy thought he had gotten away with it, but there was a witness, one he had overlooked. I had been assigned by the Feds to keep her alive until she could testify. Two days before the trial some of Tommy's boys had tried to knock the witness off. What they didn't count on was me knowing when they were coming. Three hoods went to the bad place and the witness went to court. Tommy got a life sentence and I got a flat fee.

I tried to call Cary but the line was busy and when I had the operator to break in, she said there was nothing on the line. I hustled over to his place, an old hotel on Elm

Street which had once been a speakeasy and casino, then a brothel and now low rent apartments with an even lower class of people renting them.

Cary lived on the third floor, his room in the northeast corner of the building. The place was a rat trap, the walls once a cream color now a dirty brown, the carpet on the stairs had something on it that made the soles of my shoes stick to it. The carpet in the hallway was threadbare, a couple of places showing the floor underneath where it had worn through.

I stepped up to Cary's door and started to knock. The door opened just a crack so I pulled my piece, eased the door open and stepped in. Cary sat in his old easy chair, a table holding a transistor radio beside him. A ballgame was playing on the radio, the volume turned down so the announcers could barely be heard.

Cary looked relaxed, his head leaned back in the chair, his hand still cupped where he had held the beer which was now on the floor and puddled around his feet. His eyes were glazed, his mouth open, a bullet hole in the center of his forehead, the back of it splattered on the floor. A pillow lay beside the chair, a scorch mark on it from where it had been used to muffle the sound of the pistol used. I had walked around him twice, checked his pockets and came up with nothing. I checked the rest of the apartment. The dresser had been gone through but not tossed, some of the doors on the kitchen cabinets were still open and some of the drawers.

There was a ratty old couch along the wall next to the door, the cushions had been pulled up and it had been searched. The bed, which was one of those jobs that folded up into the wall had been searched also then folded back up into the wall. The only thing that hadn't been touched was the stack of tin cans on the kitchen table. Cary was a scavenger and he collected anything that was saleable to make his rent and buy groceries.

Tin was his biggest find. He'd wander around in the service alleys behind the restaurants on Commercial Street and collect them, strip off the labels and take them to the scrap yard. I fixed the cushions on the couch and sat down, pulled out a cigar and lit up. Whatever he had wanted to tell me so bad was dead along with him. I shook my head and blew smoke at the ceiling.

Cary was one of those fellows that most people didn't pay much attention to. They figured he was just a bum and overlooked him. Cary knew this, which made his ears open and hear everything. He had come to me or Fisk with things he had heard, some sure leads, others just rumor. He had heard something this time that caused him to call me. Something that had gotten his head blown off and when I find whoever did it they were going to find out there were more ways to die than what they did to him.

I stood and started toward the door, Cary not having a phone so I would have to use the one out in the hall. I took one last look over my shoulder at the room and started to step out then stopped. A few papers fluttered in the breeze on the table from the open window and one came loose and floated to the floor. It was a label from the can, something written on it.

I turned stepped back inside and walked over, picked up the label and looked at it. There was what looked like a route drawn on it, the route going down Commercial Street to Booneville then stopped at the railroad tracks. A circle with an x on it had been drawn on the south side of Commercial Street then arrows marked its path toward the railroad tracks. There was another circle on the paper with an x in it then a square with checkmark made on it, an x on the backside. I started to put the label back on the table then paused. Pat's boys would only bag it, tag it and maybe think it meant something and by the time they did, whatever this meant would have already happened. I folded the label and stuffed it in my pocket then went out into the

3

hall and used the phone, called the Station and told the dispatcher to get hold of Pat. I had a dead body for him.

CHAPTER 1

The first thing Pat thought was the dead body was one of mine. I was on the couch when Pat and M.E. Allen Ross came through the door. Pat stopped short and Ross almost bowled him over.

"How long you been here?" he asked me as Ross pushed past him and went to Cary.

"Long enough." I stood and he motioned me out into the hall. The two of us walked toward the window facing the west in the hall. The window looked out on the back yard of the place, more a jungle than a back yard.

"So tell me about it," he said as he flipped his note book open.

"He called and wanted to see me about something and I'd say that something killed him." I flipped ash off my cigar and clamped it back in my teeth. "He was dead when I got here."

"I hate to ask because I already know. Did you look around?"

"What do you think?"

"Yeah, stupid question. Find anything?"

I shook my head no and he arched an eyebrow at me. "Nothing?"

"Would I lie to you?"

"In a heartbeat." Pat flipped his notebook shut and stowed it in his jacket, told me to stay put and he would be back in a minute. I grunted at him and leaned against the wall. Cops were all over the place and I wondered who patrolled the streets when she caught my eye. A tall blonde with a flimsy gown on, a sleepy look in her eye. The detective who talked to her wasn't looking her in the eye and I couldn't blame him, the gown was thin and accented her attributes perfectly. She glanced my way once, her eyes settled on me and a slight smile touched the corners of her mouth then she was back to answering questions and Pat came out and broke the spell.

"Any idea what he wanted to talk to you about? I mean, maybe that detective mind of yours already has a clue." Pat had his arms crossed when he asked me this. I looked up at him and grinned.

"Sherlock Holmes I ain't." I dropped my cigar butt on the floor and ground it out. "Can I go?"

"Yeah, but I may want to talk to you later."

"You know where I bunk." I turned and walked toward the stairs, Pat watching me as I went down. Out of the corner of my eye I caught the blond watching me. I smiled, winked at her and went on down the stairs.

***

I waited until all of Pat's men had vacated the apartment then went back and waited. I had checked around the neighborhood and found out she worked nights at The Horned Toad and I figured she would leave for work a little after dark and I wanted to talk to her. She had been the closest to Cary's apartment and for her to say she hadn't heard anything in my opinion was a bald-faced lie. Women have ears equipped with sonar and the slightest sound is heard by them. I should know, Shelly has them.

Around eight she came out wearing a long gray coat with a fur collar. I crawled out of the car and walked over to her before she came off the steps, stood in front of her and she stopped, a slight smile on her face and her hand inside her purse. I grinned and held out one of my cards at her. She took it, scanned it for a second and then tossed it back at me.

"I already told the cops all I know." Her voice had an edge to it and her eyes narrowed.

"But you didn't tell me." I smiled and moved up a step closer to her, my smile a nasty one which made her eyes narrow even more.

"I'm late for work." She tried to step around me and I reached up quick and grabbed her by the arm and led her down the steps.

"Then I'll take you and we can talk," I said as I pulled her toward my car, "and if I was you, I'd let go of that peashooter you have hold of. I'd hate for you to show up at work and have to explain a bruise on your arm where I took it away from you."

She hesitated and then took her hand out of the purse. I opened the door and helped her inside then walked around and opened my car door, my hand dipped first under my coat and pulled out my .45, just in case. As I slid in, she began to laugh, her hand back in her purse, something nickel-plated halfway out. She pulled it the rest of the way out and it was a cigarette case. She flipped it open and took one out, held it to her lips and I pointed to the cigarette lighter in the dash.

She leaned forward and pushed it in then said, "A little jumpy are we?"

"Just careful." I slid my .45 back under my coat and started the car up as she lit the cigarette, puffed smoke and then drew on it, blowing smoke at me and chuckling.

"So what do you want to know besides what I told the police?"

"You got a name?"

"I do. The one I'm using now is Jenny Stacks." She leaned back and let the coat fall open. The name fit the figure. She had long legs, sheathed in black fishnet hose, the cocktail waitress uniform showing a lot of thigh, the skirt puffed out and pleated. Her sweater puppies looked as if they were about to burst out of the low cut top and the cleavage was deep, deep enough to stand a pencil up in. She looked over at me and smiled, her lips full and kissable, her eyes sultry and her nose pixyish. She wet her lips with the tip of her tongue and smiled. Yeah, the name fit.

"Well?"

"Yeah," I cleared my throat and she laughed.

"Did you know Cary?" I asked the question and she shrugged.

"We only spoke in the hallway," she answered.

"He ever have any visitors?" I asked this and she shrugged again.

"If he did I wouldn't have noticed. My work keeps me out till three in the morning, I sleep most of the day unless I have company."

"You have company that day?"

"What if I did? Make you jealous?" She pushed her chest out and her balcony strained against her top, her head slightly turned and a wicked smile on her lips.

"No, makes me wonder why you didn't hear a gunshot?"

"Well, maybe the bedroom door was closed."

I grunted and shook my head. Most apartment walls were paper thin and my bet was these weren't the exception. I made a right onto Commercial and headed east, drove a few miles till I was in the middle of nowhere and then stopped. Jenny's hand started toward her purse and I grabbed it, jerked it out of her hands and tossed it out the window. She took a swing at me, her hand in claws so if it connected it would peel flesh. I grabbed her wrist and gave it a twist, her mouth twisting and her eyes going wide.

"You got two choices. One, you stop lying to me or two, I kick your ass out and you walk the rest of the way and I figure in those spiked heels, it'll be a bitch." She started to say something, her lips twisted and her eyes narrowed. I opened my door and started to scoot out, pulled her toward me and she grabbed the seat back, her mouth finally found the connection to her vocal cords.

"No, I was alone that day and yes I heard the gunshots. Then I heard someone ransacking the apartment and cussing a blue streak. I went back in my bedroom and closed the door just in case. I'm not stupid like some people are, stick their nose out and look."

"That is debatable." I shoved her back and slid into my seat, closed the door and started the car. She rubbed her wrist and gave me a nasty look and I chuckled, let the clutch out and headed toward The Toad.

"What about my purse?" She hissed the words at me like a cat. I shrugged and gave my heap some more gas.

"You know I have friends at The Toad." Her eyes were still narrowed and she was back against the door, her nasty look got nastier. I laughed and shook my head, made a right onto the dirt road that led to the parking lot and stopped.

"Out." I motioned toward the door and she grabbed the door handle, shoved open the door and slid out. I didn't wait, just slapped my heap in reverse and tossed gravel as I backed up. Jenny cussed and stepped back. One of her heels sunk in the soft shoulder and she fell and landed on her ass, the air turned blue as I laughed and sped away.

***

Pat came to see me around noon the next day, a

sheepish grin on his face as he sat down in the chair beside my desk.

"Sorry about the tough cop act," he said as he tipped his hat back. "Someone is ratting to Stills about how I handle you." I chuckled and shook my head. D.A. Ed Stills and I were not the best of friends. In fact, he says I'm a vigilante, an eyesore from a time when justice with a gun was tolerated. Times have changed he had told. Innocent until proven guilty was something that was gonna be followed. Not guilty *then* proven innocent. He swore he was gonna put me out of business and maybe behind bars so I better watch myself. Good thing I still have friends on the bench in the courthouse.

"I figured as much. What did you find out about Cary?" I asked. Pat leaned forward, dug a deck of Lucky's out of his coat pocket and shook one loose, lipped it and lit up. Once he had blown smoke, he leaned back again and shrugged.

"They found the slug," he said, "it was in one of the cabinet doors. Ross said it looked like a .357 but ballistics will have to prove that."

"And I suppose everyone on that floor didn't hear anything?"

I knew one that had.

Another shrug. "You know how it is. No one wants to get involved, especially after the papers reported on that shootout you had over on Billing's Street." I smiled and nodded. Artie Mills had written that one up. Most of it came from the neighbors in the neighborhood. They made it sound like World War Three had broken out. It was quite a ruckus though, trench guns, a Chicago typewriter and a couple of .45s. I guess it probably did sound like World War Three.

"Who was the blonde?" I asked the question mostly because I wanted to hear what Pat knew. I mean, I could have cut in with what I knew but I wanted to keep it to myself that Stacks had lied to them. Shelly, who was out at her desk yelled back, "What blonde!" I shook my head and counted to three, Shelly appeared in the doorway and stared at me. I hadn't told her about my meeting with Jenny.

"Easy kitten," I grinned. She leaned against the doorway and crossed her arms over her chest, Pat snickered and looked around at her. She was still a little upset about the last job I had worked before the witness episode. A woman bail jumper, tall and leggy and curvy. Murray Dobbs had hired me to pick her up and I had to drive to Joplin to get her. I had picked her up at the police station there and on the way back, my old heap had broken down. It had to be towed back to Joplin and we had to spend the night there, only one motel room available and cheap enough for the city to pay for.

The woman had tried to get away twice, once out the bathroom window which I was standing under, then she tried the second time by throwing perfume in my face. I cuffed her to the bed, took her clothes away from her and slept in a chair, slept light because she tried all night to get loose from the bedpost and failed. I smelled like a perfume factory when I got back to the office and Shelly huffed up. She had been talking to Gabby and Gabby had told her the woman was a slut and not many men could resist her. She also told her about me taking away her clothes. Shelly knew better but that was the clincher. I made a point to talk to Gabby when I got the chance.

"Her name is Jenny Stacks, she works at the Horned Toad as a cocktail waitress. Replaced the one who was killed. I had Wade, the detective who interviewed her to do a check. She's out of Chicago, after that, nothing."

"Sounds like someone is on the run?"

"Yeah, Andy Yates was there snapping pictures for the paper. I told him to look through them and see if he got one of her."

I chuckled. Knowing Andy, he did get one and

probably a full figure job.

"He hasn't contacted me back yet," Pat continued. "Until then I'll just have to poke around unless…"

I looked at him and smiled. His last words were a way telling me to do just what he suggested, something I was gonna do anyway. From the minute I spotted her I got a bad feeling and I always listen to those bad feelings. Pat leaned forward and flicked ash from his cigarette, his voice tense as he spoke.

"Watch you're back on this one old buddy. Stills is watching you. He'd like nothing better than for you to cross the line so he can land on you."

"Gettin' serious is he?"

"Yeah, that jumper you hauled in tried to say you jumped her bones and took advantage of her while you two were in the motel. She said you handcuffed her to the bed so she couldn't fight you off and stripped her naked. The Joplin sheriff vouched for you, told Stills she had tried the same thing with one of his deputies and she wasn't naked, just partially clothed, something he should have done when she tried to get away from them. Her lawyer tried to claim emotional duress and the judge she drew, Judge Pryor, told him it was bullshit and she would be tried for the crime she had committed post haste."

"So Stills believed the sheriff?" I laced my fingers and placed my hands behind my head and gave Pat a smile.

"Yeah, the sheriff is his uncle and he liked you. Said you had grit and Stills better not try and haul you in on a lie."

I laughed and rocked back in my chair. It was funny the way others thought of how I did things. I liked Sheriff Bates. He was a no nonsense sort of guy, old fashioned in the way he enforced the law and how he got confessions. I don't agree with the rubber hose treatment but sometimes it's the only way. I myself have never used it but I have ways, one of them is the muzzle of a .45 shoved under their chin and crazy eyes. It usually works, but not always.

Pat stubbed out his cigarette and stood, pulled his hat down and walked toward the door, Shelly stepped in so he could leave. He stopped in the doorway and turned a little, his voice taking on a tone I had heard a lot of times, his 'I know' tone.

"By the way, we checked the tin cans stacked on the table, there were ten of them, but when we counted the labels he had peeled off there was only nine. Know anything about that?"

"The window was open over the sink, maybe one of them blew off and under something."

"Maybe." Pat turned and walked out. He suspected but he didn't come right out and ask. He knew better. I'd just deny it and then clam up. When I heard the door close, I nodded at Shelly and she looked then nodded back. My fingers dipped into my vest pocket and I pulled out the label, unfolded it and lay it on the desk in front of me.

"Is that what he's talking about?" Shelly asked. I nodded and she leaned over, her balcony brushing my arm and making me think dirty thoughts. I pushed them out of my mind, the map came first, playtime later.

"Looks like a map," Shelly said as her eyes scanned it, "and part of it is missing."

"How do you figure that?"

"Right here, see these pencil marks. Someone either didn't finish it or someone tore off some of it."

She was right, but it looked like they didn't have time to finish the drawing. There was just half a square there like the one with the checkmark on it. But what was it indicating? A house, a business, a barn? I shook my head. If the coordinates on the map were right, whatever it was, was to the east of the city, way the hell east. Only a few buildings sat to the far east of town. One in particular floated into my mind and I grinned.

"I take it you've figured out what the missing half is?"

Shelly leaned on my desk and locked eyes with me as I stood and grabbed my trench coat and slid it on. "But you're not going to tell me."

"No kitten, I need to do a little poking around first, then I'll let you in on it." Shelly let out a sigh and stepped over beside me, wrapped her arms around my neck and kissed me.

"When will you be back?" she said in her sexy voice as I pulled loose. I picked up the map, refolded it and stuffed it in my jacket pocket, patted her butt and told her to keep her motor running, I wouldn't be long.

***

Kelso's bar is located on the corner of Jefferson and Commercial Streets. The entrance faces the intersection at a cattycornered angle and there is a recessed entryway before you get to the door. The insides are nice, not the usual dive like some of the other bars along the street. Kelso's is clean, no sawdust on the floor to soak up the blood from fights and the furniture isn't the secondhand type. You know the kind, ready to fall down if you sat on it. Last year he put in a pool table, bought it outright. The company he bought it from tried every way in the world to get him to rent it. That way they could get rent plus a percentage of the quarters the customers pumped into it.

Kelso told them no, he would own it and he would collect the proceeds at the end of the night and if anything happened to it there would be hell to pay. He paid cash money for the table. The delivery guys who came and set it up wanted him to take out an insurance policy on it. Pool tables could be expensive to fix and for a hundred a month, the repairs would only cost him half what they usually cost or forty percent of his profits.

Smells like a racket? It was. The company who sold it to him was also in the pinball business and connected to

Lombardo. Did Kelso buy it? Not on your life. He told the two men that if anything happened to his pool table, he had insurance of his own, the twelve gauge kind and he pulled out the Ball Buster, a sawed off twelve gauge that is fashioned into a pistol. Said men exited the bar and were never heard from again.

The night air was warm this evening, the chill was leaving and summer would soon be rolling in. I pulled off my trench coat as I walked down to the bar. As I got close, Fisk was sitting outside blowing smoke rings in the night air and watching the cars pass by.

The bench is another story. Seems that a few of Kelso's regular customers have a habit of getting falling down drunk and then Kelso had to call their wives to come pick them up. Before the bench, they had to come inside and get them which usually led to an argument and a scene in the bar. Kelso bought the bench and put it out front so that when he called a wife to come pick up their spouse, they would be either passed out sitting on the bench in a drunken stupor or slumped back mumbling about how much hell they were gonna catch. That worked for a while until one of the men, a fellow by the name of Elmo Peak, decided he wasn't gonna wait for that nag of his to come get him and he wandered out into traffic. Damned near got hit. So now someone would sit with them until the old lady got there.

Fisk saw me coming and scooted over so I could slide in beside him. I pulled a cigar out of my vest pocket and lit up, blew smoke and we just sat for a moment. Finally Fisk turned toward me, dropped his cigarette butt on the sidewalk and ground it out with his heel.

"I heard about Cary. Damned shame, he was a good kid." Fisk leaned into the corner of the bench and pulled out another smoke. "Any clues?"

I shook my head no and said, "That's why I came to see you."

"I thought it was my irresistible charm and fabulous wit that made you come see me?" He let a slight grin cross his face, something that rarely happens so I knew he was in a good mood.

"You're feeling your oats tonight, what's up?" His grin grew into a smile, his eyes sparkling.

"Remember that little blonde that was with the leather coat brigade the last time you were here?"

I nodded. That is a story in itself, one I'll tell you some other time.

"Well, we have a date tonight. She told me after what happened the night you were here, she wanted to go out with a real man, not some kid with greasy hair." I laughed, wondered if she was talking more on the line of me but didn't ask. "So who you want to know about?"

"Jenny Stacks," I said and Fisk sat up on the bench, flicked ash from his cigarette and lipped it as he talked.

"What did Pat tell you about her?"

"That her last address was Chicago, after that, nothing."

"Her last address was New York, not Chicago and she wasn't known as Jenny Stacks, she was known as Millie Truly. Her and her husband are con artists and they were running a con on an old fellow by the name of Farnworth."

"I remember that. Old guy was madly in love with her and was gonna marry her until his son figured out what was going on."

"Uh-huh, the con might not have worked but they got away with over a quarter of a million dollars' worth of diamonds then couldn't fence them. Nobody would touch them so they sent this kid they knew down into Ohio and some poor sap gave him half what they were worth and ended up beat half to death when the feds found him, the rocks not in his possession."

"Looks like he would have given the kid up?" Fisk shook his head and dropped the cigarette butt with the other and stubbed it out with his shoe.

"He did, but the kid disappeared with the money. He didn't get very far though. The Feds found him in a bus station bathroom, his throat cut and no money."

"Jenny and her husband knock him off?"

"The Feds think they did but can't prove it."

"Her husband, he have a name?"

Fisk nodded and said, "Jerry Ventura, Jr. Small time, convicted on a couple of burglary charges and served six months at Ryker's."

I nodded and shifted on the bench, flicked ash off my cigar and thought for a moment. The name sounded familiar but I couldn't place it. There was no mention of it in the Farnworth story, I had heard it somewhere else, maybe from Fisk himself so I asked.

He chuckled and nodded. "Jerry Ventura's daddy was a gambler out in Las Vegas, he was about to break the house in a crap game when the boys upstairs caught him with a set of loaded dice. He's out in the desert somewhere, coyote food."

"How did he switch the dice?"

"He had a partner, Jerry's mother. She was pregnant with Jerry at the time but only just. She had the loaded dice on her and how they switched them the boys out in Vegas are still trying to figure out."

"Like father like son," I said and Fisk nodded.

"Exactly."

"Yeah," I said and stood, shook Fisk's hand and palmed off the ten spot to him. Inflation had caused the price of information to rise. I turned to walk away and a cab pulled up, the door opened and a blond leaned out and motioned for Fisk to crawl in. I smiled and remembered I had a date myself and headed back to the office.

CHAPTER 2

After all the fun and folic, I left Shelly asleep in the bed and wandered out into the living room, the night quiet here outside of town except for a few cars that had been rodding up and down the street. A patrol car finally came by and the cars moved on to drag race in someone else's neighborhood.

I mulled over what Fisk had told me. About the con they had pulled on the old man that ended in the theft of the diamonds. Usually con men when they're discovered take a hike before the cops come and take them away, which is what Jenny did. But this was different, this was a con *and* a robbery combined. The con is the robbery in most cases but these were two separate deals. When the con failed they snatched the diamonds and then took off. Or had they had to advance their plans. Or was the con just a distraction?

I needed to find out what the diamonds were, jewelry or unset stones because jewelry was harder to get rid of, unset stones a little easier. I guess I dozed off in my chair because the next thing I knew, Shelly woke me up and handed me a cup of coffee.

"Figure it out yet?" She sat down on the arm of the chair and leaned against me, the warmth of her a better wakeup call than the coffee.

"I got some ideas." I said and sipped the coffee. Shelly had improved on the making of my favorite drink. Before when she made coffee she made it sans the diner way. Strong enough to eat the silver off a spoon.

"Well, I also had some ideas and was gonna tell you about them before the festivities started." She gave me a wicked smile and I nudged her with my elbow. I hadn't told her about the diamonds yet so I figured it was about the map. "Cary collected tin mostly behind restaurants right? And what restaurants on Commercial Street use tomato sauce to cook with?"

"Most of them but he might not have collected all of them from around here?" I cocked an eye at her and she shrugged.

"But *this* sauce is only used in one restaurant on Commercial Street. Guess which one?" She tapped the label lying beside me on the end table. I had taken it out during the night and had looked it over again. She slid off the arm of the chair and headed to the kitchen. I grinned and picked up the label, folded it and stuffed it in my shirt pocket. Yeah, there was one restaurant I would check on Commercial Street, one that used a lot of the red stuff every day.

***

Momma Jean's was two doors down from Kelso's Bar. Back in the day it had been a sandwich shop with a lunch counter and a couple of booths. When Momma Jean and her husband Poppa Joe bought it, all that changed. The lunch counter came out, part of it, about a four foot section, installed near the front entrance, the top covered in marble, the cash register on top and a bowl of mints.

The front had been installed with a glass. On the shelves installed, cigars and cigarettes sat along with some pouches of pipe tobacco in view. There was also another shelf, this one not visible from the front. Here was where Poppa Joe kept his racing form. He liked to play the ponies when he could get away with it. Momma Jean thumped his head when he didn't.

Booths now lined both walls, tables were scattered around the center of the room and red table cloths covered them with a candle in the center and other condiments around the candle. Curtains hung in the front windows, one set hung halfway up the window to give the diners privacy. That is, if the person walking outside was four feet tall.

In the spring and summer, the restaurant's front door is open, the smells of spaghetti and fresh baked bread drifting out. The door was open this afternoon and the smells assaulted my nose as I stepped in. Poppa Joe was at his usual place, his head buried in the racing form. A pencil hovered over the form and dipped every once in a while, marked a horse then poised again if he found what might be another possibility.

"You know what will happen if Momma catches you?" He jumped when I spoke, his eyes wide and his mouth open. His mouth closed and split into a grin when he saw me, his eyes reflected that grin.

"Jesus Max, you scared the hell out of me." His voice was low and his eyes cut back toward the kitchen. "I lost fifty bucks last week. Momma is out for blood if she catches me again."

"And if you had won?"

His grin widened into a big smile as he said, "Then it would of been a beautiful evening." I laughed as he kissed his fingers and tossed the kiss into the air.

"Momma around?" I asked. Joe pointed at the kitchen, the clatter of pots and pans loud from there.

"Is this about Cary?" he asked.

I nodded and he slid off the stool.

"I go get her." I pulled out a cigar and started to light it up. Joe stopped me and reached under the counter, a cigar between his fingers and a smile on his face.

"Momma, she no like the smell of your cigars," he placed a finger on his lips, "Our secret okay?" I nodded, nipped the end off of it and fired it up. It was a Cuban, the aroma rich and the taste even richer. Momma came out wiping her hands on a dish towel, a big smile on her face as she came toward me.

Momma has to weigh at least two ninety to two ninety-five. She is short, just a little over five feet tall and is a roly-poly little lady. A stained apron covered a gingham dress and her hair was piled up in a tight bun on top of her head. Chubby cheeks and a double chin fill out her face along with blue eyes that twinkle when she is happy and blaze blue fire when she is angry.

She tossed her arms around me and gave me a hug. More like a vice tightening down on a finger. She held it for a few seconds and then let go, grabbed my arms and shook me while I was getting my breath back.

"Max Black," her tone was motherly, "how long's it been since you brought that sweet little girl here to eat?"

"Awhile, we've been busy and…"

She shook a finger at me and clicked her tongue.

"Not an excuse. Too much work causes the romance to fade. When you gonna marry her?"

Momma's hands were on her hips when she asked the question. I stepped back and held up my hands and patted the air.

"Soon Momma. You'll be the first to get and invitation."

"I better. Now what do you want to see me about?" She grabbed my arm and led me to a back table where we sat down, the noise from the kitchen muted but still there.

"When was the last time Cary collected tin cans from behind the restaurant?"

I could see the gears turning in Momma's head and a

finger tapped her lips.

"Last Wednesday. I wash the cans before he picks them up and I was finishing the last three while he collected the others."

"Did you talk to him?"

"I was going to, but this man he come along, drunk as sin he was. Stumbled around in the service alley. Cary seen him and went to help him. He brought him over and grabbed up his sack, told me he would be back later."

"So he knew the guy?"

"No, but Cary was a kindhearted soul. Did you know he had a drinking problem?"

"No," I shook my head. I guess my eyes widened a little because Momma smiled.

"We all have secrets Max. This one Cary shared with me one time when he was collecting cans. He had almost, how you say…"

"Fell off the wagon."

"Yes, he was about to fall off the wagon. He found a half bottle of ouzo that had been hidden behind one of the crates out back." She leaned over and gave Joe a look. "I took it away from him so he wouldn't be tempted. I also had a talk with someone about the ouzo."

Ouzo is a Greek drink of which Poppa is half and he does like to indulge every so often so yeah, I figured the talk was where Jean held a club over his head and told him if he did it again, the club would fall. As to the fellow he was helping out, I leaned back in my chair and puffed on my cigar, blew smoke at the ceiling and asked, "This fellow he helped, you get a look at him?"

"I did, but it was dark and his face wasn't too visible. He was tall and skinny, not boney, just skinny. He had on an expensive suit, a little rumpled and dirty, but you could tell it was expensive. His face was long, his nose long too and he had dark hair, oiled down like they used to do back in the thirties. His eyes I didn't see but when he looked my way I got an uneasy feeling."

I nodded and tapped ash off the cigar into an ashtray and patted Momma's hand then stood. She stood also and followed me to the front door, Joe stuffing the racing form away under the counter and Momma gave him the eye.

"Thanks for the cigar Joe and thank you Momma for the information." I stepped out, hesitated in front of the window and acted like I was relighting my cigar. Out of the corner of my eye I could see Momma, the racing form in her hand and Joe dodging it every so often.

***

So Cary was an alky. He didn't look like the usual boozer. You know the type, the fall down, skin their nose off on the concrete drunk. No Cary looked normal anytime I had talked to him. Oh, I had smelled the booze on his breath a time or two but I figured he had a little nip to ward off the chill in the air. Shelly's Uncle Carl was a drunk, a mean drunk. She told me a few stories after I had met the fellow, the smell of cheap scotch heavy on his breath.

He was a mean and sloppy drunk, staggered around in the house and destroyed just about anything in his path and if he ran out of whiskey, then he got meaner. Her Aunt Ella had been his punching bag when his bottle went dry. Telling her how useless she was and how he should of married Deedee Stone, now there was a woman. If she mouthed back, he beat the hell out of her.

He had tried that on their visit back here. The bottle of scotch he had guzzled down sending him off into a rage, yelling and swinging, Ella catching one on the nose and breaking it. The next thing he remembered was his ass draped over the rail of the back porch, me sitting in a chair waiting for him to come to and knock his ass out again if he went off. He was just sober enough to know better and stumbled to the chair beside mine. We had a talk that night, one that ended in if he didn't get his life straight, he was either gonna be dead by Ella's hand or by some young punk who would beat him senseless, steal him blind and leave him in the gutter to bleed to death.

I thought maybe it had taken but I should have known better. Carl ended up in a ditch just outside a factory in Detroit, his pockets empty and his head caved in. I hate it when I'm right. Ella did get him to go to Alcoholics Anonymous before his death and he did straighten out for a while but it didn't last. A week short of a month he went on a binge and that was when he was killed.

The local chapter of AA met in the Mission on Campbell Street, the building a homeless shelter owned by the Catholic Church in the city. It had once been a storage warehouse and when the man who owned it died, his wife deeded it to the church, mostly because she didn't want to pay taxes on it and it was a big deduction on her taxes at the end of the year after she gave it to the church.

Father Mason runs the joint, the good Father almost as rough as the people who come in to have a clean and dry place to sleep. He stands a little over six feet tall with snow white hair and a mustache to match. His face is square jawed, heavily lined and his eyes are a piercing blue that cuts into a man the minute he locks them on you. One of the winos I know says all he has to do is lock those eyes on you and you'll tell the truth no matter what.

The meetings were on Tuesdays and Thursdays and this being a Thursday I figured I would drop by, maybe talk with Mason and find out if Cary had any friends he hung around with. It was around seven when I walked in, the signs told me that the meeting was held in the back room of the building and entrance was at the side door. Inside the door a fellow who looked like he was seventy years old met me, asked my name so I told him and before he could pin a tag on me I told him I was here to see Father Mason about Cary.

He informed me that I would have to wait, that the meeting had started and Father Mason officiated. I told Gramps it was ok, I'd wait. About ten or fifteen men were grouped in a semi-circle in the center of the room, seated in folding chairs and listening to a fellow tell how bad a boy he was until he stopped drinking. A few of the fellows I knew, some of them big wigs in the city. One I knew quite well. I took a seat in the back of the room so they wouldn't see me and listened.

Around nine, the meeting broke, Father Mason saying a prayer and then the men picked up the chairs and cleaned up. I guess he had spotted me during the meeting and came back to where I was, waved off a couple of men who wanted to talk. He strode over to me and stuck out his hand, gripped it and gave it a shake.

"I suspected you would come see me sometime." His voice was low and he looked back at the men cleaning up. "Best for those in the room we go back to my office. Some of them might not be too comfortable if they saw you."

I chuckled and nodded as he led me to a small room off this one, more like a closet than a room, the only thing in it being a desk, a file cabinet and a couple of chairs, the file cabinet having a more than a few dents in it.

"I call this The Venting Room," he waved an arm around the room. "The only furniture in here is a desk, chairs and an old file cabinet. If someone becomes agitated, the chairs are replaceable along with the file cabinet."

I settled into one of the chairs and it creaked and groaned like it was gonna give any minute but held. I pulled out a cigar and offered it to him. He shook his head and reached into the desk and pulled out a box, flipped it open and nodded toward it. Inside were Perfectos, Cuban and dark as dirt. I took one, thanked him, nipped off the end, lit up and offered him a light after he had done his. We sat in silence for a moment, a light cloud of smoke filled the room and Father Mason laced his fingers and put them behind his head as he leaned back in his chair and looked at me, the cigar clenched in his teeth as he spoke around it.

"You know anything Cary told me in confession is confidential?"

I nodded and blew smoke at the ceiling and said, "So what can you tell me that isn't?"

Mason grinned, took the cigar out of his mouth and spoke.

"He came to me one night after a meeting and said he had a problem. A fellow he had helped was going to do something bad and he didn't know what to do. If he went to the cops, this fellow would be mad at him and in trouble, if he didn't, then someone might get hurt."

"Did he tell you what this fellow was planning to do?"

Mason shook his head and said, "I tried to get Cary to tell me what it was but he told me it was better if I didn't know but he did show me a drawing."

"You remember what it looked like?"

"I may look old and feeble Max but I'm far from it. It was a map scribbled on a tomato can label. I asked him again what it meant and he just folded it up and stuffed it in his pocket, shook his head and started to leave. I stopped him and told him he needed to go to the police and he shook his head no again. I then told him he might talk to you and he just turned and walked out. I guess he did talk to you."

"I was too late." I flicked ash off in the ashtray on his desk. "I was in court that day." I reached in my pocket and took out the map, unfolded it and lay it on Mason's desk.

"So how did you get this?" He gave me a sly look, picked it up and looked it over.

"Remember what you told me about confessions being privileged?"

He let a smile grow on his face and said, "So I did."

"Consider how I got it in the same fashion."

Mason laughed and handed the map back to me,

flicked the ash off his cigar and leaned back again.

"This drunk, did he bring the guy here?"

"He did, but that was before he came to me at the meeting. Do you think he was the one…?" Mason leaned forward and shook his head. "I gave him some money and told him to take him to Benny's and sober him up, then bring him back and we would see what happened. When I saw Cary again, I asked if this fellow was with him and he said no then told me what he did."

"You get a look at the guy?"

Father Mason rocked a little in his chair, the springs in it squealed as he did.

"I figured him to be just a wayward person out on a hoot. Cary was always a kindhearted soul and figured any man who was drunk was an alcoholic. I figured once Cary got him sober, the guy would thank him, tell him he was just having a good time and leave."

"You remember what he looked like though?"

"Tall and skinny, not bony skinny, just thin. He had on a nice suit that I suspect would have to go to the cleaners the next day and expensive shoes. He had a long face and a long nose. His eyes were what bothered me, even drunk, they had a predator look to them, like he wasn't someone to fool with and his hair was black, slicked back like they used to do back in the thirties. The smell of that God awful Tiger Root hair oil stunk up the air."

I stood and started to leave, then turned and asked, "Cary, how long had he been an alcoholic?" Father Mason looked at me, the smile faded and a sad look came into his eyes.

"Since he was a young boy. His father ran out on him and his mother when he was a baby and his mother, being a young woman had a hard time coping. Cary told me a woman who had known his mother told him that he cried a lot when he was a baby, colic, teething, so his mother who liked the gin bottle, spiked his milk to quiet him down. It worked but it also turned him into what he had been. He almost died three years back, the doctor who treated him drying him out instead of turning him loose to do it over again. In fact, the same doctor comes to these meetings. He was here tonight at this very meeting."

I nodded and thanked him, exited the building and walked down to the corner of Commercial and Campbell to try and catch a cab. A lot of home remedies were used back in the day for all kinds of ailments, some of them working, others doing nothing. My own mother had rubbed whiskey on my gums when I was teething, just a drop on her finger not a shot in my milk. It was a wonder Cary wasn't dead. No wonder he was a little slow, Bathtub Gin made with God knows what back then. Bottled and corked and sold at a premium price, the stuff sometimes killing adults if it wasn't made right.

By the time he was six he was already a drunk and years of sucking up cheap booze only added to the problem. As to the doctor who saved him, yeah, I seen him at the meeting and would have more respect for the man after this. I might even quit fiddling with the murder victims until he got there.

CHAPTER 3

Cabs were a little on the lean side tonight so I decided to walk, the air a little chilly but not bad. What Father Mason had told me rolled around in my mind as I headed back which was probably why I didn't observe the two most important rules in the PI business. Rule number one; never hamper your gun hand. Rule number two; never walk close to the mouth of a dark alley. Rule number one is a given for me, my trench coat always loose enough for me to dip my hand under it and my jacket. Only a couple of times have I been lax in this rule.

Rule number two popped into my mind when I was in the middle of the dark alley opening. I had just started to give the blackness a wide berth when a pair of hands came out and grabbed me but not good enough. I stepped back toward the street, the hands grabbed a sleeve and my other hand dipped, my .45 jumped out and the other hand grabbed my wrist. I jerked my arm and the hand that held the sleeve turned loose, the other hand tried to twist my wrist and get me to drop my .45. The action didn't work.

Instead I took another step, this one to the side and I

turned, the step quick and the hand holding my wrist loosened so I could turn my pistola in the arm's direction. Just as I pulled the trigger a body came out of the blackness, slammed into me and my shot went high, but not high enough. There was a scream from the darkness and a body fell to the sidewalk. The other one came up off me, swung and would of connected hard with my jaw if I hadn't of jerked my leg up and caught him in the back, his fist scraped the side of my head then concrete.

I gave him another knee in the back and he howled but didn't roll off. I started to do it again and he got lucky, his fist connected with my chin and little stars swirled. Another fist almost closed the curtain and I figured that was it…until I woke up with Pat looking down at me, a smile on his face and Ross telling someone never mind, I was awake. Ross helped me sit up and my head, which barely throbbed now throbbed harder, each boom in my ears like a bass drum in a marching band. I groaned and looked up at Ross who wet down a cotton swab and dabbed at the cut on my chin.

"Playing with the bad boys again." Ross dabbed at the cut. I grunted, pushed his hand back and tried to get up and didn't make it. The ground moved which made my stomach lurch and almost expel supper. I eased back down and Ross snickered.

"You know, it was a good thing I was in the neighborhood or you might be in a bag like the other one."

"So I got one?" I asked the question in a raspy voice and Ross nodded.

"Right in the head, not a between the eyes shot but a little to the right, just over the right eye. Same effect though, in small, out big."

"What about the other one?"

"He was about to cave you're head in when I jumped out of my car and pulled off a shot at him. He has a bullet in his body somewhere, probably in the arm or side. I've already contacted the hospitals about it."

Suddenly it hit me and my hand went to my jacket pocket, the only thing it held was lint. I cussed which was not a good thing to do, my voice made the booming louder. Pat came over about then and both he and Ross helped me up, Pat helping me out to his car. Ross told him I should go to the hospital and stay the night. Observation. I growled out a no and crawled into his cruiser and told him to drive me to Shelly's. Ross started to protest and Pat waved him off, told him to forget it, he knew who he was dealing with and crawled into the cruiser with me and took off.

I swear, I think Pat found every pot hole and rough spot in the street. By the time we got to Shelly's I was ready to show him what it was like to be roughed up but didn't have the energy. He helped me out of the car and into the house, Shelly grabbed me and helped him get me into the bedroom, my head pounded, nothing a few aspirins couldn't fix. I took three and when Shelly tried to take the bottle, I growled at her and she let go.

The conversation in the living room between them drifted in and out, Pat telling her to watch me, some hood had tried to beat my head in. If she answered I didn't hear her and the next thing I knew she told him bye and was easing herself down on the side of the bed. I mumbled I was sorry and popped two more aspirin then handed her the bottle which she recapped and set on the nightstand.

"One of these days Max…" Her voice faded and the booming became less and the curtain fell.

***

I woke the next morning with a knot on the back of my head the size of a grapefruit. I looked at the clock and it was half past eleven so I started to get up, my head swam when I did and Shelly was beside me in a heartbeat.

"You need to rest." She pushed me back. "That hood

tried to cave the back of your head in on the sidewalk."

"Who told you that?"

"Pat, he said Ross kept the bum from killing you."

"Yeah, I owe him."

"Big time." She stood and told me to just take it easy, she would bring me some coffee and if I felt like it some breakfast. I said okay and she disappeared into the kitchen, appeared with a mug of coffee and helped me sit up so I could drink it. She hadn't fallen apart this time like she did before. I noticed she was slowly getting used to me getting hurt. As of late it was more often than not. As I sipped the coffee she stood from the bed and puttered around the room, her emotions settled some by doing it. Maybe it was time for me to hang up the harness.

I had been debating it for the past few months now. I was getting older and a little slower lately. I was still fast on the draw, but my other motor functions just weren't as fast. Like how I forgot to give the alley mouth a wide berth. That was something I always did even in the daytime. Other things were prevalent also. My legs, which in this business are a necessity, were stiff sometimes in the morning as were my hands. I had to work my fingers to get the kinks out and loosen them up.

I had gained weight, ten pounds on my six foot frame and I was feeling it. We had talked about this a few weeks back, Shelly telling me she thought we should tie the knot before some hood made her a widow before she wore a ring. This time was close, too close.

"Remember what we talked about a couple of weeks ago?" She sat back down on the side of the bed and smoothed my hair down. "You know, about maybe taking Jack on as a partner?"

"I remember."

"Well?"

"Well what?"

She started to punch me in the arm then stopped and

gave me the eye.

"About taking Jack on as a partner and it's a good thing you're hurt or I would have put a hurt *on* you."

I laughed, another thing that wasn't so smart to do but I couldn't help it. Shelly has a hell of a temper when she gets aggravated and a punch in the arm is usually how she expresses it.

"Yes, I've thought about it. When's he coming home?" Her face lit up when I said this and she smiled.

"A week from tomorrow. How long will it take you to teach him what you know?"

"Oh, probably awhile, maybe a year or two, depends on how fast a learner he is," I said tweaking her chin. She gave me an evil smile and leaned in close, her lips brushing mine as she said, "I'll tell him to learn quickly."

I chuckled and she stood, smoothed her dress out and walked to the doorway, her hips doing the shimmy.

"Are you hungry yet?" She looked over her shoulder and batted her eyelashes at me.

"Always." I winked at her. She giggled and exited the room.

***

I was supposed to be resting. As you can guess it wasn't going to happen. The coffee had helped me perk up and I took a few more aspirin and waited till she got busy. Shelly was in the kitchen tossing pots and pans around while I showered, scraped some stubble off my face and got dressed. I slipped out of the bedroom, grabbed up my trench coat and hat and made for the door, Shelly realized what had happened as the front door creaked when I opened it and headed for the car. She was on the front porch as I pulled out of the drive her eyes drilled holes in my heap as I shifted into gear and made haste as the poets say toward my office tossing her a wave. I'd catch hell over it but I had things to do.

Once there, I called Ross and asked if the man he had wounded had turned up. He told me no, but the word was still out. I thanked him for being there and he said no thanks necessary, just keep what I knew to myself and I told him my lips were sealed. I hadn't eaten yet, my exit skipping breakfast so I locked up and headed to Benny's. My head hurt a little, especially when I put on my hat but that was better than being dead. I owed Ross one.

I was halfway to the diner when Pat pulled up and screeched to a halt in the street. I walked over and he told me to crawl in. I hustled around and opened the door, a delivery truck behind us honked and the driver leaned out the window and cussed a blue streak. Pat grinned at me and hit the siren. I looked back and the driver sat still for a moment, his mouth open and his eyes wide. We both laughed as Pat pulled away headed west on Commercial Street. He made a quick trip to the corner of Grant and Commercial then pulled off into Pop's gas station. He said Ross's gunshot victim had been found.

Pop had died back in 1947 and his son had sold the station to a fellow who owned a couple more in the city. The independent owner turned into a franchise owner which meant the gas prices rose and fell depending on what company was trying out sell the other. A guy in a white uniform stood talking to a patrolman, a grease rag in his hands wiping them as he talked. Pat and I crawled out and we walked up to the patrolman who, when he saw us coming, stepped back and nodded.

The guy was no more than a kid of twenty-one, his hair red and his face so pale the freckles on it stood out like measles. Pat questioned the kid while I walked over to where a couple of Patrolmen stood by the grease rack, the current owner building a cinder block building around it. It was lowered and a couple of flood lights on in the pit beneath it, another add on by the owner since the rack had developed a leak and the new owner, instead of fixing it, took out the piston and dug a pit, leaving the rack in place and bolting it to the concrete edges of the pit.

Down in the pit was a body slumped against a tool box; the lights turned the blood pool around him black. It was the hood Ross had shot. He had gotten as far as Pop's, knew he wasn't gonna make it and crawled down in the pit to breathe his last. I walked down a few steps, paused and lit a cigar then started to go on down when someone behind me cleared their throat. Ross came down beside me and paused also, then went on down and across to the body. I leaned against the pit wall and watched.

"The bullet went through his side." Ross lifted his arm and pointed. "Probably punctured a kidney and then exited the back close to his spine."

He dropped the arm and started to go through the hood's pockets, turned them inside out and found nothing more than lint. Pat stepped up beside me and looked at me, Ross shrugged his shoulders and stood and walked toward us.

"He took something out of your pocket just before I fired, he was about to finish the job when I did." Ross gave me a questioning look then looked at Pat, Pat folded his arms across his chest and glared at me.

"So what did he take?" His voice was low and had the cop tone to it. I looked at him and motioned for him to follow me. Once out of the pit, I led him to the gas station's main room and leaned against the counter. Pat stood in front of me, his eyes glared into mine as he tapped his foot and waited.

"That label you've been missing," I said around a cigar that was clamped in my teeth, "I lifted it from the apartment and before you throw a fit, I haven't figured out what it was too yet. I have an idea but that is all." Which was a little white lie but he didn't need to know that. I took a ticket pad off the counter and tore off one, flipped it over and with the stub of a pencil drew what was on the label.

"Looks like a map." Pat eyed the drawing and then eyed me. "But to what?"

I shrugged and switched the cigar from the left to my right side of my mouth and said, "That is the million dollar question. Part of it is missing but I think I know which part."

"Tell me."

"There were marks on the end of the original, someone tore part of it off or just didn't finish the map. This is outside the city. Only a few buildings on this end of Commercial Street. Until I'm sure I'm right I think I will keep it to myself."

"If Stills finds out you even think you know…" Pat shook his head and I grinned around the cigar.

"He doesn't have to. Just tell him I fell to the evil of a couple of bad guys who wanted to end my nosey ways and you ran across this when you searched him."

"I take it you've been checking this out?"

"Every chance I get."

"And what have you deduced Sherlock?"

I told him what I suspected but not what I knew and he shook his head.

"Pretty thin. Cary could have drawn this to remember where he had stashed his cache of cans."

"That far outside of town? And have you ever known Cary to stash anything? Plus, the street names are spelled correctly. Since when did he become a spelling bee champ?"

Pat nodded slowly, folded the ticket and stuffed it in his pocket. The gears in his head were deciding whether to ask the next question or not. Depending on the question, I have a habit of sidestepping things like if I had a lead. He went ahead and asked anyway.

"Something tells me this involves Lombardo and his bunch. Is that true?"

I grinned and took the cigar out of my mouth and rolled it between my fingers, then clamped it back between my teeth, took out my Zippo and relit it. This took a few minutes which makes the red start crawling up Pat's neck because he knows I am stalling.

"Well?" he growled at me as I blew smoke.

"To be honest, all I have is hearsay and the description of a fellow Cary helped before he was killed. Nothing concrete. As to it involving Lombardo and his crew, I couldn't say either way."

"Or won't." Pat grunted and glared at me. The red had rose to his ears and the grunt was a nasty one. He knew damned well I wasn't gonna part with what I had and no amount of needling or rubber hose treatment was gonna get it out of me. He pointed a thick finger at me and his voice was low and tight as he said, "If Stills ever finds out you have withheld evidence, which I know damned well you are, you'll be so deep in the jail that it will take flood lights to find you."

He turned and walked away, back to the red headed kid who was still talking to the officer and wiping his hands. I bet he had the cleanest hands he had ever had since working here.

CHAPTER 4

Shelly was at the office when Pat let me out in front of it. When I walked in I expected an ass chewing and got just that. The girl is an expert when it comes to bitchin' me out. If we ever have any kids, they will soon learn not to do anything stupid or her barbed tongue will lash them and make them feel bad for doing whatever they have done. Of course I have become a little immune to this over the few yeas we have been together but it still stings.

I just listened until she was done, nodded ever so often and when she ran out of steam, kissed her on the forehead and made haste back into my office, dodging the swipe of her hand at me which meant she was cooling down some. I slid out of my trench coat, tipped my hat back on my head and sat down at my desk, took a sheet of paper out and redrew the map, picturing in my mind, knowing what the missing piece of the map was and knowing in a roundabout way what they were up to.

I called a friend of mine, Brian Cutter who worked for the only armored car company in the city. After the war he came back and got a job with them and a year later was working behind a desk planning the routes of the four trucks that picked up around the city. The business was growing and he had at least added three more armored cars to the fleet. I asked him if they had any pickups outside the city. He said no, most of the businesses were small on the outside, the only one which might and did generate any amount of money would be the Horned Toad and he said I knew for damned sure they didn't use their service. I laughed, thanked him and hung up. Now I maybe knew what they were up to. They being Jenny and Jerry.

The Horned toad was owned by Frankie Lombardo, the head cheese of the rackets here in the city. Small by New York and Chicago standards, a little fish in a big pond, but little fish sometimes become sharks and from what I had heard, The Horned Toad drew people from all over the four county area which made Frankie look good. Gambling and vice were the main dishes there. The games crooked, the prostitutes in abundance. A lot of the city hotshots made tracks out there at least once a week either to gamble or bed down a favorite.

The Toad sat just outside the city limits, a long, ranch style home that had been added onto when Frankie took it over. There was a gravel parking lot on the south side of the building, the only way to get to it being a dirt road off the highway going west and ending at a set of railroad tracks. I've never been inside. I'm not too welcome there, but I hear it is a showplace.

I looked down at the map and with a pencil, drew in a square where the one was missing. The circles with the x's in their centers were stops, they had to be. But stops where and for what? The what I had a good idea of. At one time, Lombardo had wire services and loan shark setups all over the city. Pat and his boys had tried to sniff them out a time or two, but the sniffing turned out to be a snort, the businesses moved, nothing there but a few tables and cigarette packs crumpled up and tossed on the floor. Then things changed, the Feds got involved and most of Frankie's wire rooms and loan shark businesses bit the dust, some of them anyway. I hear he has a few well hidden and they shut down for a while until the Feds got tired of hunting.

I leaned back in my chair and locked my fingers behind my head. The what was money. Hard cash that was handled and bundled and picked up maybe once a week or sooner if it got to be a large amount. I smiled and nodded to myself. Someone planned to hit Lombardo's money makers, but probably not one at a time. I suspected the square with the checkmark on it was the place where the full kitty was dropped off, counted and then shipped out.

The circles were the pickup points but there were no buildings drawn across from them, not like the last one with the checkmark on it which meant the circles were the pickup points. If there was a wire service or other racket on this street I hadn't heard of it but that didn't mean they weren't there. I reached over and picked up the receiver of the phone, dialed the Station and asked the switchboard if Pat was in. They said he had left for the evening, something about an urgent appointment. I grinned and wondered if that urgent appointment was Gabby. If it was, what I had on my mind could wait. I got up and stepped out into Shelly's office to tell her I was going out to snoop around a bit when the phone rang. Shelly answered it and then handed it to me.

"Your buddy Ross, he said it was important." I took the phone and put it up to my ear, Ross talking to someone with his hand over the receiver. I gave it a three count and then said hello.

"Max," Ross said across the wire, "the guy we found down in the pit? Pat got an ID back on him."

"So why didn't he call?" Ross grunted and told me to hang on. I could hear him talking to Pat, this was the urgent appointment, and Pat growled okay and there was a thump as the phone was lain down and then another thump as it was picked up.

"I just called the Station and they said you went out on urgent business, is this it?"

"Yeah, the guy Ross whacked, we found a laundry mark in his clothes and when we checked it, it belonged to Jerry Ventura but that doesn't mean it's him. I took a set of prints and am gonna run them to make sure." Pat's voice was low and serious as he spoke.

"What about the map?" I asked a question and there was silence on the other end for a few minutes then Pat spoke.

"The map wasn't on him. There was also another hole in him, this one in the same place as the Docs. Docs exited the guy but this one was still in him. It's a .357, like the one that killed Cary."

I let Pat hang on the wire for a few minutes, rocking back and forth on my heels as a smile crossed my face. I wondered if the blond in the apartment was the one who put another slug in the body and grabbed the map.

"Max!" Pat's voice was harsh and I chuckled into the phone.

"So you want me to come down there?" I asked

"No, I've seen enough of your ass for one day." Pat's voice had a raspy note in it, the same note he has in it when he is aggravated at me. "Just thought you would want to know."

"Yeah, thanks," I answered him as the receiver on the other end clicked and a dial tone buzzed in my ear. I hung up the phone and stood still for a moment, my hand rubbing my chin, Shelly cocking an eye at me.

"What?" I stepped toward the door.

"That look." She said it like it was a nasty thing and I grinned.

"Don't wait up kitten," as I opened the door and exited the building.

***

I pulled up in front of the apartment building around seven and crawled out of the car, the super on the front stoop sweeping it off, his wife leaning out a window and giving him hell. She looked like hell. All three hundred pounds were stuffed in the window, her hair in curlers and an old housecoat covered her bulk. Her face was twisted in the womanly rage that most women have when their husbands are not listening to them. God I hope Shelly never gets that look. She was telling him he needed to get on cleaning out that dead guy's apartment today. It had set empty far too long and the longer it sat empty the more money they lost on it.

He nodded as he swept, the words came out of her mouth a mile a minute, the super's ears closed to the sound. I got to the bottom step and she caught sight of me, her face like a predator cat's, ready to pounce if I said the wrong thing. I smiled and tipped my hat to her, the face never wavered and a grunt came up out of her massive weight as she pulled herself back in the window and slammed it shut. I walked up the steps and the super, a short balding man with shaggy eyebrows and a cookie duster under his nose.

"Thanks buddy," he said as he swept the last of the dirt off the stoop. "Sooner or later I would have had to answer the old warhorse and the fight would have been on. What can I do for you?"

I pulled out my folder with my PI license in it and flipped it open. The super scanned it for a minute and then looked at me and nodded.

"I remember you. You were the one who found Cary." He opened the door and motioned me to step inside. "Damned shame about Cary. He was a good kid, a little slow but a good soul. I suppose you want to look around in his apartment?"

I shook my head no and asked, "The blond woman who lived in the apartment across the hall from Cary's, she at home Mister…"

"Banks and no, she don't even live here anymore."

I gave him a questioning look and he shrugged.

"She moved out yesterday. Some slick looking guy helped her. I don't think they got along too well. She cussed him under her breath as he hauled her luggage out to the car and was giving him thunder when they pulled away."

"You hear anything she said?" I pulled a fin out of my pocket and waved it in front of his eyes which widened along with a smile on his face. He reached for it and I pulled it back, shaking my head and smiled back.

"She called him a stupid asshole and said something about a map. That he better get his shit together or everything would go to hell in a hand basket." He reached for the fin again and I shook my head again.

"Only two fifty's worth." I folded the fin and started to slide it back in my pocket. "You're gonna have to do better than that."

"He told her everything was under control so to quit bitchin. The boss had the map."

"The fellow who helped her move, what did he look like?"

Banks stood for a moment, his eyes half lidded, the gears turning in his head.

"Tall guy, skinny, not boney skinny, just skinny. He had on an expensive suit, one of those tailored jobs and his shoes were Italian leather. His face reminded you of one of those Ferrets, long and sneaky looking. He had dark eyes."

"The blonde, she say where she was going, a forwarding address?"

"Nope, she didn't get any mail anyway."

"You ever see her and Cary being buddy, buddy before he was killed?"

"Not that I know of. Besides, my old lady has a jealous streak. She thought I was watching the upstairs I'd be sleeping on the front stoop." He said this with a shake of his head and a shrug. I knew how he felt. I've been accused of things like this by Shelly, nothing to keep me from sleeping in the bed but usually it is a cold bed until she calms down.

I handed him the fin and he stuffed it in his pants' pocket, glanced at the door to his right and chuckled.

"The old lady finds out I got a fin on me, she'll shit."

"Our little secret. Have you cleaned out her room yet?"

"Not yet, I was gonna do it after I cleaned out Cary's place."

"Mind if I look around a bit?"

"I don't guess it could hurt. She in trouble?"

"Probably." Banks nodded and we headed up the steps to Jenny's room. As he unlocked it, I stood and looked at Cary's door. From where I stood, if the door was open you could look right into the kitchen where the table was and the cans were stacked. From here she could see the table and since she was being nosey she could have seen me pick up the label. I grinned and made a note in my head. Banks unlocked the door and stepped back and around me headed toward Cary's room.

"Okay, let me know when you are done. I'm gonna go see if I can get the blood up off the floor. Probably have to sand and re-stain it. The blood gets down between the boards and in the wood grain. You can't get it out so you just..." he stopped, a dopey grin on his face as he turned and walked away. What he was doing was no secret. All apartment managers did it along with other tricks to spruce an apartment up for the potential renter. It was later that they usually found out what was hidden in the cracks of the floors or the patched spot on the wall.

I swung the door open and stepped inside, the smell of perfume and face powder strong in the dead air. She had cleaned the place out well, just a few scraps of paper scattered around, the dresser drawers empty and the closet the same. Even the bathroom was as void of left behind woman's things. I went back out to the living room and stood for a moment, then walked over and sat down in the easy chair by the window.

She had a good view of the street out front and the chair was comfortable, the seat sinking down some when you settled into it. What was it Fisk said, she was a cocktail waitress at the Horned Toad? I shook my head and chuckled. Jenny was there to case the place out, to get a handle on how much money the casino took in every night. Nope, no con here, but a heist that if pulled off would net them a trunk load of money—if they could get away with it and live.

We're talking about the Big Boy's money. Green that financed their other operations. Money that belonged to them and them alone. You steal it, you might get to enjoy some of it until they caught up with you, then it was concrete overshoes or a bullet in the head, take your pick. Of course, if you were lucky, you might be able to disappear for a few years under an assumed name, maybe have a little face work done to extend your living years. In the end though, they would get you, they always did.

I started to get up and as I did more than just face powder and perfume touched my nose. I smiled and stood, walked to the door and opened it, the smell of Tiger Root hair oil coming from the chair I sat in still warmed my nose.

***

Pat's boys occupied the second floor of the Station. The room looked small with all the desks crammed in it and his office sectioned off in the back half. It was an 8x10 cube, one desk, a couple of file cabinets, three chairs, the straight backed variety and a lot of paperwork stacked around. It looked like my office and it felt like home. A few of his detectives were just coming in. These fellows worked the night shift, four of them, two youngsters and two seasoned detectives to keep the younger ones from screwing up.

Harcord and Ames were the seasoned boys, both of them having been detectives when I first hung out my shingle. Ames was close to me and waved me down, a smile on his face as I walked up to him.

"Plan on talking with Pat?" His smile grew wider when I nodded. "Might want to stand in the doorway and knock first."

"He still pissed?" Ames nodded. I pulled a cigar out, clamped it between my teeth and stepped out in the aisle. "He'll get over it."

Ames laughed and I walked on down to Pat's office, stood in the doorway and rapped on the door. He ignored me at first, his head down then his eyes cut my way. I grinned and raised a fist, Pat's head jerked up and a snarl came from his lips. "What!"

I held up my hands in surrender and stepped in, Harcort and Ames snickering.

"Just came by to clue you in on what I think the map might be about."

Pat grunted and leaned back in his chair as I slid into the one by his desk, lit my cigar and puffed smoke.

"Well?" His voice was tense and I grinned around the cigar.

"I have a feeling it's a robbery of the casino Lombardo runs way out on East Commercial."

"And how did you come to that deduction?"

"I called Stanton's Armored Car Service. They make no runs outside the city."

Pat dug around on his desk and pulled out another file, flipped it open and took out the map I had drawn him, looked at it and then looked at me.

"You could be right." Some of the tension slipped from his voice as he spoke. "But like I said before, it could be a map of where Cary stashed tin at. The Toad does have a restaurant."

"True, but can you see that bunch letting him collect the tin they throw away? Also, that is too far for him to travel, especially lugging a load of cans."

"I can see your point," Pat sighed, "but who…"

"Jenny Stacks has also vacated her apartment lock, stock and face powder."

"So?" Pat eyed me and I leaned toward him. "Rumor is she was in on the diamond heist of that old man in New York. She and Ventura was running a con and it turned sour so they boosted the diamonds and split."

"And had a hard time fencing them," Pat said with a sigh, "I've heard the story. The kid they hired to do it was supposed to be connected. He was but the diamonds were too hot and nobody in New York wanted to mess with them. The kid took them out of state, Ohio, and a fellow there took them off his hands for a third of what they were worth but the kid took off. Jenny and Jerry left without a pot to piss in."

I nodded then asked, "So how much did the kid get?"

"Five grand, the stones were worth three times that. The state police recovered most of the set jewelry except for three stones, diamonds as big as your thumb."

Evidently he didn't know about the kid being found with his throat cut. I kept that to myself.

"And they were the most expensive is my guess?" I asked him and he nodded.

"Yeah, over a half million dollars and get this, rumor is Lombardo has secured the diamonds."

I let out a low whistle and leaned back. Now we know who slit the kid's throat. If Jenny and Jerry were gonna do what I think they were gonna do and they could get away with it, they could disappear for a very long time. Pat leaned toward me, his eyes locked with mine as he said, "You got that look."

"What look?"

"The one that tells me you got an idea of what might be going on."

"If I told you, would you give it a few days before you did anything?"

"Depends on what it is?"

"Uh-uh, I want to catch the piece of crap that killed Cary plus get the diamonds back and give you Lombardo in the long run."

Pat sat and thought for a few minutes, the gears in his head turned as he debated whether to do what I asked. Then he nodded.

"How long is a few days?" He asked the question and then wished he hadn't. A slow grin spread across my face around my cigar and I chuckled.

"A week," I answered. Pat half closed his eyes and groaned as I added, "It will take me that long to narrow things down."

"Okay Max. A week, I'll stall Stills off as long as I can but I want you to keep me informed."

"Will do." I said this and Pat shook his head, mumbling the hell freezes over bit under his breath.

I stood, smiled around my cigar and stepped toward the door, Pat watched as I did. I stopped and turned back toward him, the cigar clamped between my teeth as I said, "You won't be sorry."

"I already am."

I stepped out the door and headed toward the exit, the four night detectives watched me and talked as I stepped out on the landing and walked down the steps.

CHAPTER 5

I sat in my office and ran things through my mind; the street outside quiet, a few cars passed once in a while and a few lovers strolled down the street. In the bigger city there would always be a low growl of noise, distant cars and trucks, their tires howling on the pavement, a horn or two blaring out at some knucklehead who had cut them off. When I first moved here, the quiet didn't set with me too well. I was used to some kind of noise on the streets. Now, it was kind of nice, gives a guy time to think and concentrate.

Right now I was concentrating on Jenny and Jerry. This wasn't only about money. This was about getting back what had been taken from them also. The kid may have gotten away with the money and the fence may have been busted but the three diamonds, they had ended up back here and probably in Lombardo's hands. Jerry and Jenny, or Millie or whatever the hell her real name was had gotten wind of where the diamonds were and had tracked them here.

But the map was still the puzzle. If Frankie had the

stones he would probably keep them in his safe out at the casino. That is unless he was selling them. Or maybe they were coming in? I leaned back in my chair and smiled. Maybe the diamonds were coming in when the money went out. If that was the case it would be a double payday. But to do that, the two of them would need a few more men. A heist like that would have to be well planned.

I stood and grabbed my trench coat, slid into it and headed for the front door. I almost got to it when the phone rang and I was almost out when Shelly yelled at me and told me it was Ross. I told her to take a message and she told me he said it was important. I grunted and came back in, took the phone from her and growled into the receiver.

"It better be good. I've had an epiphany." There was a chuckle on the other end and Ross spoke.

"I didn't know you knew big words like that. I thought tough guys didn't use that kind of English."

"We ain't all illiterate. What's on your mind?"

"That hood I popped. Pat called and said he wasn't Jerry Ventura."

"I was just there, how come he didn't tell me then?"

"He said he tried to catch you but you had already left. I told him to call you and he growled something about indigestion and asked me to relay the news. He was talking low when he told me."

"I bet that indigestion was a fellow by the name of Stills."

"That's what I figured."

"So who was he?"

"A guy by the name of Preston, local fellow who has been in and out of jail most of his life. What's the deal with you and Pat?"

"Stills. The shit is on his back about me."

"So that was why Stills called him on the carpet."

"Say again?"

"Rumor is Stills called him up to his office this

morning and I guess shredded his ass big time. I understand
that Stills wanted you brought in and charged with
withholding information and obstruction of an
investigation."

"Is that a fact?"

"Uh-huh, Pat stood up for you and said if it hadn't
been for you a lot of these cases you had worked with him
would still be unsolved. Stills informed him that this wasn't
a Wild West town anymore. That he had better tell you to
stick to taking pictures of cheating spouses and tracking
down bail jumpers or he was gonna slam you so far back in
jail you'd never see the light of day."

"His exact words huh?"

"So I was told with a few embellishments added."

"Thanks Ross. Call Pat for me and have him meet me
at Benny's in about an hour. I got some things to tell him.
If Stills is there he has a habit of grabbing the phone from
Pat if he thinks it is me on the other end."

Ross laughed and said, "Will do."

I hung up and stood for a moment. Shelly watched me
close as I shook my head and then walked to the door, gave
her a wave and stepped outside. Stills was coming up for
election this year and he was suddenly playing hardball.
But why now? Till lately he had been just a thorn in my
butt, a small pain that I usually ignored. Something else
was brewing here and if I had my way, I would find it.

I walked down to Kelso's and slid into Fisk's booth.
He sat and looked at me for a few moments, a half smile on
his face as I told him what I thought the Ventura gang was
up to.

"Makes sense," he said with a small shrug, "but
snatching money from the big boys will get you nothing but
trouble, we both know that."

"Not if it was done before Lombardo and his hoods
found out about it."

"You mean like someone on the inside."

"Exactly. Someone close to the counting room."

"Or close to the delivery man." Fisk nodded and rubbed his chin for a moment, his eyes narrowed as the gears turned in his head.

"The delivery man is Manny Hull. He's been with Lombardo for a long time. There is a new driver though, fellow by the name of Fairmont. He came down from Chicago about a month ago. His credentials were good so Lombardo gave him the job."

"Out of Chicago huh?"

"Yeah why…" Fisk's grin grew wider and he let out a low whistle.

I checked my watch and stood, palming off a ten to Fisk and told him to keep an ear out. I hustled down to Benny's, my favorite diner, Benny on his favorite stool with his nose in a detective magazine. I waved as I passed him and walked down to where Pat sat in a booth along the wall, slowly stirring his coffee and looking like he had been kicked in the butt. I slid in across from him and he looked up, a half smile crossed his face and he leaned back in his seat.

"Why didn't you tell me Stills was kicking your butt because of me?"

He shrugged and said, "I figured I could handle it, I have before but this time something is wrong. This time he is on the warpath. He threatened to have my badge if I didn't arrest you the next time you withheld information. I told him he could have it anytime and he told me to hand it over. If it hadn't of been for Chief Niles, I'd be out of work. Niles told him he didn't have the authority to take my shield and Stills went berserk. Told him he had the right and would see that it was done. I may be looking for a job after today."

"I wouldn't count on it old buddy." I smiled. "I got connections Stills don't want to mess with. Besides, I have some things to tell you, hypothetical but probably pretty close to the truth."

I spilled what I thought was going down and Pat sat and listened, nodded his head every once in a while and took it all in. We sat silent for a moment, the gears turning in his head as he thought about it.

"Something like that would have to be well planned." Pat looked at me. "Plus the fact that it would have to be kept close to the cuff. Your man hasn't gotten wind of any of this?"

"I just talked with him and no, he hasn't but that doesn't mean he won't find out."

"You'll keep me informed this time?"

"This time for sure. Look, don't worry about Stills, he'll back off after I call in a few favors."

"Thanks Max. For the life of me I can't figure out what has got into Stills. He was ranting like a madman."

We talked a little more and Pat said he had to go check in with his people and then poke around some more. I told him to take care and watched him walk away. All the times he had coved my ass came to mind. All the ass chewing's he had taken because I had stepped over the line. Now it was my turn to return the favor. I grinned and slipped out of the booth, headed toward the front door when I saw the car. It was a black Ford, the snout of a trench gun poked out the window as Pat walked down the sidewalk. I didn't even think, just drew my .45 and let go, the front glass of Benny's shattered as slugs slammed through it, the trench gun roaring, Pat falling, the Ford trying to speed up. I aimed, fired off two and the car swerved, bounced off a pickup and slid to a stop.

I hit the front door just as the trench gun man crawled out, his face bleeding as he raised it and then his head exploded like a ripe melon as I put one between his eyes. I ran across to the car, the driver slumped over the wheel. I growled a curse and shoved him back, his eyes glazed, a red flower blooming in his upper chest. It was a lucky shot and I wished I hadn't been so lucky. I'd liked to have had at least one of them to talk to.

I let him slump back and ran back to where people were gathering around Pat who was getting up off the sidewalk. I grinned at him as he brushed off dirt from his coat and then someone handed him his hat. We both looked at it and started to laugh. The top of it was completely gone, another inch and it would have been his head.

***

Once everything was said and done, I herded him back to my office where I took out a bottle of Jack Daniels and poured him a stiff one. He knocked it back and held out the glass so I poured him another.

"You saved my ass buddy," he said after he drank half the Jack, "if you hadn't of fired through the window..."

"Yeah, I've got to tell you though, those two were not part of Lombardo's crew. I know most of Lombardo's boys and those weren't his."

"Jerry's boys?"

"Probably. I figure Jenny is running this one. I had Shelly do a check on Jerry. He was the one who muffed the diamond heist, Jenny had it down solid and it took him twice to crack the safe. One of the maids came in on him just as he got the safe open. He cracked her skull before she could scream but he didn't crack it hard enough. She got out a yell and he almost got caught going over the fence. The brother was the one who accused Jenny of being in on the deal and had her arrested. She made bail and then jumped it."

"And ended up here." Pat let out a sigh and set the glass down on my desk, his face serious as a parking ticket. "What I want to know is how they tracked the diamonds?"

"Connections my friend. Probably people who owed her favors or she got the info out of them by other means."

I arched an eyebrow a couple of times and Pat snorted. Remember, I had gotten a good look at her and figured it wasn't beneath her to ruffle the sheets to get a guy to talk.

"Well," Pat stood and looked over his hat, the whole top of it was gone, "I guess I better check in with Stills. He informed me that if I got any information to contact him *immediately.* Of course I don't have to tell him about what you told me, just about my near death by trench gun." He had a grin on his face and I chuckled.

"I think some of me has worn off on you buddy?"

"God I hope not." Pat had a big grin on his face when he said this as he turned and walked toward my office door. I grinned back and he walked out, speaking to Shelly as he left, her body appearing in the doorway as soon as the door thumped shut.

"Something ain't right," Shelly said as she leaned on the door jamb.

"Isn't right." I corrected her. "Tell me what you think *isn't* right?"

"Don't be a smartass." She walked around behind my desk and leaned on it, her skirt hiking up a bit and a firm thigh appeared. "Eyes forward buddy."

"Sorry lady, let's have it."

"Jenny making tracks right after Ross killed the man that tried to kill you. If it was me, I would lay low till things cooled down. In my opinion, she knows when the diamonds are coming."

"You mean like someone on the inside might be the one who tipped her off."

"Yeah, I mean if Lombardo already had the rocks, he would have them safe somewhere. I think they are planning a double take down, both the money and the diamonds when both reach the delivery point."

I didn't have the heart to tell her I had already thought of that but if she had the same idea too then it was possibly a sure thing. I just needed to prove it.

"Very good kitten. You're learning."

"I have a good teacher." She slid off the desk and kissed me on the cheek but before she could get away, I grabbed her and pulled her into my lap and kissed her hard and sweet before she could get away and head back to her office before someone walked in.

***

Jimmy Bell is a war veteran. Three Purple Hearts, a Medal of Valor and a Silver Star. A hell of a lot of good it did him though because his last wound in the Big One was to the head, a sniper bullet hit him in the temple and for some strange reason followed the curve of his skull and came out the top but not without doing some damage. He wasn't fully off his nut but he had bad days, sometimes the jacket squad was called out and he spent a couple of days in the nut ward at City Hospital.

Most of the time though he was okay. Today was one of those days. He was standing in the alley between the Citizen's Drug and May's Fine Fashions. I gave the alley mouth a wide berth since the last incident and almost walked past him because he was back in the shadows. He let out a low whistle and I stopped.

"Got a minute Max?" His voice was low and he leaned forward to look up and down the street. I nodded and stepped into the alley with him, one more look and he ducked back in.

"Someone after you Jimmy?" He shook his head and I thought maybe he was having one of his bad days but his eyes were too bright and he was breathing regular. I reached in my vest and pulled out a cigar, held it up to him and he took it. He usually lets me light him up after I give him one but this time he slipped it under his coat and shook his head.

"For later. Right now you need to know something."

"What?"

"You got a tail on you, a good one. He's been on you since you snuffed the two in the car."

I took a cigar out and clamped my teeth down on it, rolled it from one side of my mouth to the other and leaned out to take a look. Across the street was a fellow in a tweed suit, a brown fedora and an umbrella under his arm looking at the display in one of the store windows.

"You see him before?" I asked.

"A couple of times," Jimmy said, both of us watching him. "Once in Benny's and once in The Cove. He talked to a redhead, tall and leggy, she had a big balcony with a deep center aisle."

"Did you hear what they were talking about?"

"Conn ran me out before I could get close enough. The bastard told me if I wasn't buying to get the hell out. But I did hear her call him Mr. G."

"Thanks Jimmy. You doing okay?"

"Yeah, how about you?"

"Just capitol old buddy, just capitol." I slipped a fin in his pocket and walked down to the other end of the alley, came out on the back side and walked down to the alley beside my building. At the mouth of it I stopped, looked out and saw Mr. G. looking around. I chuckled and went back the way I came, walked all the way down to Jefferson Street and took a left, watching down the street as I entered Kelso's and smiled.

CHAPTER 6

Kelso's was pretty dead. Only a few of the regulars were in attendance. The jukebox was playing a Glenn Miller tune and a couple of old timers were knocking balls around on the pool table. I walked over to where Fisk was seated and slid in across from him. He looked up at me and then back down at the beer in front of him.

"Back again huh?"

I nodded and then asked, "Don't tell me I'm bad for business?" I nodded toward the room and Fisk grunted.

"No, Stills is." The words came out of his mouth like he had tasted something rotten and if Stills was involved, it was. "He came down here and tossed his weight around a couple of hours ago. Said he was inspecting all the bars here in the city. Looking for underage drinkers and he said that a little bird had told him we patronized some. He checked everybody's ID and then told Kelso that if he wanted to keep his license *he* better not be serving beer to minors. Then he came over to where I am, said my day was coming. He knew I was a snitch and he didn't like them unless they worked for him. I told him I was just a patron and nothing more. He just smiled and leaned down real close and told me I'd better watch who I told things to. I might wind up in the pen."

Pat, now Kelso and Fisk. Shelly was right, something was wrong but I just couldn't wrap my head around what it was.

"So what you want to do?"

"Same as always. That prick is into something and I've got people out trying to find out what it is."

I leaned forward on the table and Fisk looked up at me, his eyes narrowed and his face tight, his hands clenched in fists so tight they shook a little.

"You sure?"

Fisk nodded and relaxed a bit, his face softened up some but the fire still burned in his eyes.

"Sorry Max, the asshole needs to be cut down a notch."

"He's on my list to do that. Now, tell me about a fellow called Mr. G?"

Fisk leaned back and took a drink of beer, swallowed and then leaned forward again, his face back to normal, serious and to the point.

"Mr. G. is a man who plans things. He's been arrested in most of the major cities with no convictions. His last gig was down in Dallas, an armored car hold up, none of it tracing back to him."

"How much did he net out of the job?"

"A couple of hundred grand, but none of it found. They say he's got connections with the mob and they launder his money for a certain percentage."

"Which means he comes up on the short end."

"Yeah, they say he has a very high lifestyle so he plans these jobs to keep himself in that lifestyle. I take it you've spotted him?"

I nodded and said, "He's been tailing me and he's good at it. Jimmy told me about him."

Fisk leaned back and let out a low whistle, tapped the

beer glass with his finger then leaned forward again.

"He's casing you out Max. Why?"

"I think I know but I'll keep that to myself, for now anyway." I stood and shook Fisk's hand, the usual ten spot passed between us and I walked to the back of the bar, slipped into the storeroom and out the back. There is another alley between Kelso's and Mama Jeans, I slipped down it and peeked out at the street. Mr. G. was walking down the opposite side, looking around like he didn't have a care in the world. I chuckled and ducked back down the alley, made tracks back to the office and stepped inside, leaned against the door and waited.

It took him five minutes before he passed my door. I knocked on the glass and he stopped, turned and looked at me. I grinned and gave him a wave and he tugged down his suit coat and took off. Shelly was in my office and came out after he passed. She asked what I was laughing about.

"A tail I gave the brushoff." I took off my trench coat and hat. "From now on, keep the door locked and your .38 cocked okay? Anyone who resembles a hood you put lead in them and head for the back door."

"Maybe I oughta upgrade my artillery," She smiled and went over to one of the file cabinets, opened it and took out her other piece. I grinned as she strapped her .357 revolver under her arm. When I bought it for her, we went out to a friend of hers who owns a farm. After about a month, she got to where she could hit better with it than the .38 but it was a heavy gun and she only wore it in an emergency.

She settled the pistola under her arm and then asked me what was going on. I told her about my talk with Fisk about Mr. G. Then I turned and locked the door, went back in my office and called Pat.

***

I met him at a small restaurant up on the square. It was a hole in the wall place which mostly catered to the beat generation, a few of them already there sipping coffee and smoking. They didn't pay much attention to me when I walked in but when Pat arrived, a few of them slid out of their seats and headed for the exit. I knew the owner and he gave me a look and shook his head. The girl that waited on us asked if we might be leaving soon, the owner said we were bad for business. I told her to tell him not to worry, we weren't here for a bust. She smiled and took our order and in a few minutes came back with two steaming mugs of coffee.

I told Pat about Mr. G. and he nodded. He had heard the name before, had gotten some bulletins about the man a year or so ago.

"I can get a file on him if you want," Pat said and sipped the coffee. It was black as coal and bitter, the usual sugar container wasn't on the table and he made a face. "You can probably get more than the file says with your connections."

"I already have but I'll poke around some more, Stills riding your ass still yet?"

"Yeah, I'm beginning to think you're right, something isn't right."

I leaned back in my chair and paused for a moment. Could Stills be involved somehow or was he riding Pat because an election year was coming up? It could be either one but my mind suspected the latter. Come this November the voters would be going to the polls and knowing Stills, he wanted some notches in his belt before that happened. I was about to say something else when a uniform came through the door. Heads jerked toward him and a few more feet hit the floor and exited the building.

"Captain Peterson?" Pat nodded and the uniform swallowed hard and glanced at me. "There's been a shooting down on Commercial Street, a woman…"

I was up and headed toward the door, Pat behind me yelling. I didn't hear him, the words 'a woman' echoed in my ears as I headed toward my car.

***

Two bodies lay in the doorway. One man had a hole in his chest and the other had the top of his head missing. I stepped over them and into Shelly's office, my kitten sitting at her desk, Ross working on her arm. When she saw me she started to get up but Ross pushed her back and told her to sit still, he would be done in a minute then she could hug me all she wanted.

I watched while he worked on her, a nasty bullet burn on her arm, Ross dabbed antiseptic on it and Shelly cussed under her breath. When he was done he stood, gave me a chuckle and walked over to the dead bodies as I slid around him and looked down at Shelly, her hands in her lap, gripped tight together to keep them from shaking.

"So what happened?" I asked. She took in a deep breath and let it out slowly, her voice a little shaky as she talked.

"I was in your office when I heard them come in so I stepped into the doorway and asked if I could help them. The one in front asked if you were in and I told him no. He smiled and said good, less trouble in handling me and then he took a step forward. I drew and fired, his eyes wide as he looked down at his chest and then back at me. The other one was still in the doorway and was aiming so I fired again and his eyes rolled up and he fell across the other one."

She took in another deep breath but this one hitched a couple of times so I pulled her toward me and held her close. She didn't exactly cry but the tears were misty in her eyes and she was holding on to keep them from falling. Shelly has killed before, but not up close and personal. It's always a shock to the system when it happens that way. Guys usually get sick, the fear of just escaping a bullet churning up what is left in their stomach. I doubt it was any different for women. Shelly looked up at me and wiped her eyes, sniffed and then took off, the churn in her stomach winning out.

Pat came through the door a few minutes later, stopped to talk with Ross and then came over to me.

"Ross said she was lucky." He jerked his head at the two on the floor. "I bet those two are from out of town."

"And you'd probably win," I said as Shelly appeared, Pat helping her to sit down and asked if she was able to tell him what happened. She did and he glanced at me and I smiled. It was her first baptism of fire from close range and she seemed to be weathering it well. Tonight after the adrenalin wore off would tell whether she would be alright. I was about to ask if she would be alright and go look at the bodies when a voice from outside touched my ears and made me cuss.

Stills stepped into the doorway, his hands on his hips as he inspected the scene. He has the face of a bulldog, pinched and lined, his head bald and his lips rubbery. His eyes are pinpoints in his face, not from fat but from the bulldog look. He is average height but stocky built, his suit well-tailored to fit his frame. His shoes are expensive and shined to a mirror finish. His shirt was a light gray but his tie is a purple-blue. Edith Head would be ashamed. He never said a word, just looked things over and stepped past the bodies. His eyes settled on me and a sneer crossed his face.

"Some of your work Black?" He spat the question out like a father talking to his son after the son was caught doing something he wasn't supposed to.

"Depends on what you call work." He had locked eyes with me and I locked back, his prosecutor's stare good, but not good enough. After a couple of minutes he looked away and I chuckled, red starting to creep up on his neck as he looked at the revolver on top of Shelly's desk. He took a pencil from the pencil cup and slid it down the barrel, brought it up to his nose and sniffed.

"This has been fired recently." He looked up at me and I shrugged. "Yours?"

"Could be." He glanced at me and then at Shelly.

"Yours?" He asked and Shelly nodded.

"You did this?" His eyes narrowed and he took a step toward her. "Take this woman into custody Captain Peterson."

"That won't be necessary." Pat said. "Witnesses say it was self-defense. One of them came at her and she defended herself."

"Witnesses huh. You have statements from them?"

"My people are getting them."

Two of the older uniforms were digging notebooks out of their pockets and heading toward the crowd. Stills gave him a stare then looked at Shelly, her face tight and her eyes narrowed as she stared back. Like me she didn't crack under his stare and he grunted and looked back at me, the red having spread all across his face.

"So who are they?" he growled at me.

"Don't have a clue. Newbies would be my guess."

"Why would they want to kill your secretary?"

I looked at Shelly and she shrugged. Stills grunted again and turned to Pat.

"I want a full report on my desk by tonight. As for you…" He tossed up his hands and headed toward the door. If he had of been a steam engine he would have already popped a safety valve. Ross was bagging up the bodies as he stomped toward the door, Wendell in his way. He growled for him to get out of the way and Wendell grinned, told him to hold his horses, he would be done in a minute. But Stills wasn't going to wait a minute, he pushed past Wendell, his shoe catching on one of the body's arms. I suspect the arm was moved on purpose, and he stumbled out the door. Wendell looked at me and winked as he and Ross finished zipping the rubber bags up and hauled them out to the car.

***

I was right. When the adrenalin wore off Shelly broke down, not serious, but she asked a lot of questions, most of them about how I felt when I killed my first. I told her I was a cop then. A couple of hoods were rousting a storeowner, beating him because he didn't have the right amount of protection money to pay them. I told her back in those days, a lot of cops just turned a blind eye to this. I couldn't even though my partner told me to.

I bulldozed in, kicked some ass till one of them decided to end it and pulled his piece. I didn't even think, just drew and fired as I dove for the floor. He screamed and grabbed himself, his days of fathering children over. The other one was still grabbing for his piece, had it halfway out and I plugged him twice in the chest, his eyes wide as he looked down at the two holes in it and then fell on his face.

Did I get a commendation? No, I got talked to, told how sometimes things just couldn't be helped and that it was best to just let it slide. Later I was told that there was a price on my head and I better make tracks because the blind eye was already on me.

"But how did you *feel?*" she said in a soft voice. I sat for a moment and thought. That was a long time ago and I've popped a lot of bad guys since then. I looked at her and shrugged.

"That was a long time ago babe. I remember feeling fear for my life and later, that verse in the Ten Commandments popped into my mind for a while, you know the one, 'Thou Shalt Not Kill'." I figure the guy upstairs turns a blind eye to someone who deserves it." I leaned back and looked at her. Shelly nodded and then curled up beside me. I tossed an arm around her and held her as she told me it was the look in their eyes, the 'I'll be damned' look, then their eyes glazed and she knew they were dead.

I nodded and she snuggled in tighter against me. If it didn't make her stronger it would haunt her for the rest of her life and that haunting would be bad. I've seen folks who have killed someone in self-defense and have it follow them, make them careless and being careless in this business would get you dead.

I held her till she was asleep then laid her out on the couch and settled in the easy chair, lit a cigar and let things roll over in my mind. The two goons I figured were sent by Mr. G. to shut me down. I suppose they were told not to kill Shelly but to mess her up a bit, a warning for me to back off and turn a blind eye.

What he didn't know was Shelly can take care of herself and his goons found out the hard way. Besides, if she hadn't of gotten them and they did mess her up, no rock would be big enough for them to crawl under. I would find them and make them wish they hadn't messed with her. Especially Mr. G.

Then there was Stills. Pat was beginning to catch on to what I suspected all along, that something wasn't right. That the election wasn't the only thing that was keeping him riding Pat and trying to push me out of the picture. Maybe it *was* the election.

I'd need to check with a few friends down at the courthouse to see if maybe he was hiding something. I was about to stand and get Shelly a cover when the phone rang. I flipped the receiver off the cradle and answered it. It was Pat. He said I needed to come down to the Station before Stills had me picked up.

I told him I'd be there and hung up. The sound of Stills

voice in the background made me curse under my breath, grab my trench coat and fedora and head out the door.

CHAPTER 7

The squad room was empty, not a living soul sat at the desks. The only ones in the room were in Pat's office, Stills who was slamming the air with his hands and Chief Niles sitting beside Pat's desk staring. Pat saw me coming down toward them, his eyes cut back to Stills before he got wise and I walked up to the door, grabbed the knob and shoved it open. Both Stills and Niles jumped. Stills halted in midsentence, his arms still in the air.

"Well, well, you do come when called?" He had an 'I got you look on his face' when he spoke. I smiled back at him, shrugged then said, "If you had of called I would of told you to stick it. What's up?"

"The gun those men were shot with, I checked the gun. It was reported stolen a few weeks back." He had a Cheshire cat smile on his face. "You bought it from a fellow you knew, a Milt Booker?"

"Yeah, he said it belonged to his brother and his brother wanted to get rid of it. How did you…"

"I memorized the serial numbers on the gun. Did you know this same gun was used in a robbery, one that wounded a man down in Joplin? I guess you've finally screwed yourself. Possession of a stolen weapon, buying stolen property, my, my, what do you think is going to happen next?"

"Nothing," a voice spoke from behind him. Stills spun and stared into the eyes of a good friend of mine, Judge Perry Carter.

"Judge Carter I…" Stills voice was a high whine. Carter flinched and used a hand to wave Stills off before he could say anything else.

"There has been a mistake made here." He handed Stills a piece of paper. "Max called me earlier and said there might be a little trouble with the pistol. Seems it *was* reported as being used in the robbery in the beginning but then the officer who reported it was trying to cover his ass because he was part of the robbery. Seems this Milt's brother had registered the gun because he was a part-time deputy for the Joplin PD. The officer involved in the robbery also had a gun of similar make. He just switched the guns when his brother wasn't looking."

Carter held out a file and Stills looked the papers over in it, then muttered something under his breath then looked up at Carter. Carter had a big smile on his face. I had checked the pistol out before I had bought it and it was just as Carter had said. Milt's brother, being a superstitious soul, didn't want the piece around. He said it was tainted by bad mojo. Stills grunted at Carter and then turned to me, the steaming, red face was back and I do believe I actually *saw* steam coming out of his ears.

"One of these days Black you'll screw up big time and I'll land on you, you bet your sweet ass I will!" He shook his fist at me, his fingers so tight the knuckles were white. Stills whirled and stomped out of the room, muttering to himself as he went. Niles stood, shook Carter's hand and said he had to be going and exited the office. I looked at Pat and we both laughed.

"I called Carter before I got here, had him check to see if anyone had called in a check on Shelly's piece." I shook Carter's hand and he shook his head.

"What's put the burr under his saddle on you?" Carter asked. I shrugged, took the seat Niles had been sitting in and tipped my hat back.

"That's what me and Pat have been trying to figure out along with what may be a heist involving mob money and diamonds." I said as Carter settled in another chair.

"You mean the Farnworth diamonds?"

"How do you know about those?"

I have connections too Max." Carter leaned back and smiled. "Three perfectly cut diamonds, insured for five million. The old man who had them has offered a five hundred thousand dollar reward if they are returned. This reward is on the sly though since he has filed a claim with the insurance."

I let out a low whistle and Pat muttered a damn.

"There is also another fellow in town who wants to get his hands on them." Carter took out a deck of smokes and shook one lose, offered and when we declined, he lipped one and fired it up. "His name is G, just G, I hear he wants the diamonds for the reward. I also hear that Lombardo has acquired the stones, but not yet in his possession. I also hear that Jenny and Jerry Ventura are after them as well. This could be quite a party when it comes together."

Carter chuckled then stood, took another drag from the cigarette and then ground it out in the ashtray, walked to the door and then stopped as he gripped the door handle and said, "Got a minute Max?"

I nodded and stood. Pat gave me the eye and I grinned at him, shrugged and followed Carter out the door. Halfway to the squad room exit he stopped and turned, his voice low as he spoke.

"A tip for you. Jenny Stacks is staying at a boarding house over on the south side of town, Jerry has disappeared for the time being. He is wanted for assault of the Farnworth maid. I understand they had a little falling out over the map he drew for the kid that was killed a few days ago. She told him she wasn't going to take the fall for a murder and she split. I suppose if you questioned her, she might give up Jerry boy to you."

I nodded and Carter walked down the center aisle and disappeared onto the landing to the stairs. I stood for a moment and thought about what he had told me. I wonder who his connections were. I looked back at Pat and he shrugged. I walked back and leaned on the door jam, Pat waiting for me to speak. When I didn't he grunted and leaned back in his chair, his eyes narrowed.

"Something I should know?" His voice was low, almost a growl and I grinned around the cigar in my mouth. He muttered a curse and waved a hand at me, went back to fiddling with the papers on his desk and muttering to himself as I turned and headed toward the steps.

***

The boarding house was on South Street, one of those old two story jobs that had survived the Victorian age. It was weathered but didn't look trashy, the shutters were all in place and only a few spots showed peeling paint. The owner had put in a parking lot in the back, a gravel job which sported two cars and an old garage, junk stacked in it and spilling out the front door. I pulled around back and saw a sign that said entrance.

I crawled out and walked up the back steps onto the back porch, knocked on the weathered screen door and waited. I was about to knock again when a little old lady came up to it. Through the screen she looked to be over eighty, heavy set in a housedress that had seen better days.

"Ain't got no rooms," she said in a raspy voice, the smell of booze almost knocked me down when she spoke.

"I'm not looking for a room but if I may, I'd like to speak to Miss Stacks if she is in?" The old gal cocked one eye at me and looked me over for a moment then smiled. She had about three teeth left in her mouth and her eyes sparkled as she chuckled, the booze on her breath smelled like gin.

"You must be a cop. Jenny told me to watch for cops and if they came to let her know."

"I'm not a cop."

"So what the hell are you then?"

"A private investigator."

"Same damned thing."

"Look granny, tell her I'm sorry for the way I treated her the last time we talked but I need to talk to her again." My voice had a little edge to it because I was tired of playing twenty questions with the old woman. She grunted and thought for a minute then opened the screen door and motioned me in. We went through the kitchen to the front room, the kitchen spotless which usually is a mess in places like this.

"I keep a clean house," she said after catching me looking around. "Someone makes a mess anywhere in this house and they find themselves lookin' for a new place to live." We went into the living room, a big parlor set up with a couple of couches, two easy chairs and a rocker. I suppose the rocker belonged to her because there was knitting in the seat and a sign taped to the back that said 'Hands off If You Want to Live'.

"Be just a minute. I'll go up and get her," the old woman said. I nodded as she mounted the stairs and went up. I gave the room a look over and noticed one the sofas looked funny, too far away from the wall. I stepped over to it and looked. The body of a woman was tied up and tossed behind it. I ran to the front door, out onto the porch, the sound of a door being slammed on the left side of the house. I rounded the corner and a stairway from the second floor led down to the yard. A blonde carrying a small suitcase came down the steps fast. The steps were an open framed job so I ran under them and when she reached the second step from the bottom I reached out and grabbed her ankle, the woman screamed and she pitched forward onto the wooden landing at the bottom. I came around fast, Jenny already on her hands and knees ready to bolt and run once she got on her feet.

I reached out and grabbed a hand full of hair, the idea was to keep her off balance and yank her to her feet so I could get ahold of her before she could try and get away. Didn't happen. I grabbed her hair and gave it a yank. The hair came off her head and the yank was a hard one which caused me to get off balance. I staggered back, caught myself just in time for her to bolt forward and ram her head into my stomach.

I decompressed and fell backwards, trying to suck in air. She was a little off balance after the head butt too so I rolled over on my stomach and tried to grab her ankle again as she staggered backwards. She spun and was headed away from me so I came to my knees and started to get up. I had forgotten about the old woman. Suddenly I saw stars and colors, the colors and stars rolling around like a kaleidoscope as I fell forward, the colors and stars fading, then blackness.

***

I woke to the smell of grass and dirt clogging my sinuses. There were also voices, faint but getting louder.

"He's drunk," one voice said.

"He ain't either," the other voice answered.

"How do you know?"

"Cause there ain't no whiskey smell on him."

I groaned and the two of them jumped. A couple of boys probably between seven and ten. I rolled over and they took a step back. I couldn't see their eyes but I figured they were the size of silver dollars. I sat up. The two about to take another step back when I asked, "You two live around here?"

"Yeah, in the house next door."

I reached up and felt the back of my head. A lump just behind my ear as big as a goose egg was there.

"Go get your dad," I said as I flinched when I touched the knot. "I need him to call the cops."

"You heard him," the short one said. I'd got a better look at them and one was about six inches shorter than the other.

"Don't tell me what to do." The tall one's voice was defensive as he growled at his buddy.

"One of you just go," I rasped out as I tried to stand. The tall one took off, the other one tried to help me up but my legs wouldn't hold me. I dropped back to my knees and groaned again. In about five minutes the kid and his father came toward me, the man tall and broad shouldered. He knelt beside me and asked if I was alright.

"Besides the knot behind my ear I think I'll live," I said. He chuckled and helped me up, my legs holding me up somewhat as we walked across the yard to his house. Once inside, he yelled for his wife, a tall skinny woman with red hair and freckles. She came into the kitchen and stopped short, her eyes narrowed and her hands going to her hips.

"Who the hell is he?" she said in a guarded tone. I reached in my coat, pulled out my folder and tossed it on the table. Her husband picked it up and flipped it open.

"He's a private cop. What the hell happened to you?" His voice was defensive as he lay the folder back on the table and looked at me.

"I'm on a case. The old woman who runs the house over there whacked me upside the head and helped one of her boarders get away from me."

"Old woman huh?" He looked at his wife and grinned. "The one who owns the house isn't no old woman. Sally is a red head like my wife, probably around thirty. She runs the place with her sister who's out of town. I suspect the old gal who conked you was Willie Morris. She used to be a floozy back in the day. Ran with a fellow by the name of Gammon, a bootlegger. She was rough back then and still is. Here let's get this wet coat off you and Mary can take a look at that knot, right Mary?"

He looked at her and Mary shrugged. I stood and he helped me off with my coat, the trench wet. At first I figured it was dew but from the look of it, there had been a shower and had soaked the coat good along with my pants. Once that was off he liberated my jacket and then let out a whistle.

"Some artillery." He nodded at the .45 under my arm and I nodded back which I wished I hadn't of.

"I like 'em to stay down when I hit them." I grinned up at him and he nodded his head.

"That will do it buddy. I was in the war. Carried one of those for a while. Wish I had of smuggled it back with me because, like you said, they stay down after they are hit."

"Are you two finished?" Mary was standing beside us, a bottle of alcohol and a couple of washcloths in her hands.

"My name's Dan and as you know hers is Mary," Dan stepped back and let his wife step behind me. She doused the washcloth with alcohol then dabbed at the knot and I flinched. Dan stepped around in front of me and pulled out a chair, sat down and looked me over for a moment.

"Yeah, I remember you. Your picture was in the paper when Russo and his boys went down. I hear that was quite a show."

"Yeah, it was."

"So what's Sally into I mean are you looking for her?"

"No, one of her boarders, tall blond headed woman. At least I thought she was blond."

Dan gave me a puzzled look and I smiled.

"I tripped her up trying to catch her and was going to try and keep her off balance by grabbing her hair but it wasn't *her* hair. She head butted me and knocked the wind out of me, then granny whacked me with a club."

"I take it she got away?"

I nodded and he chuckled.

"Yeah, I seen someone take out in a dark blue Chevy, 1951 model. They tore out of here fast, two of them in the front seat."

"One of them the old woman?"

"Couldn't tell, they were hauling ass. All I can tell you is they were making tracks back toward the city."

I nodded and Mary told me it wasn't a bad knot, might be hard for me to wear a hat for a while but I would live. I grinned then looked at the two boys taking all this in.

"How would you two like to make a buck a piece?" I asked them. Faces lit up and the boys moved closer. "I had a hat. You find it and the wig and you each get a buck."

Feet hit the floor running, some shoving and name calling ensued as the two made tracks back over to the house. Dan and I laughed and Mary shook her head as she walked away. I leaned back and closed my eyes for a moment, the throb in my head was low but would probably build once I got to moving around. When I opened my eyes Dan was watching.

"This Sally, she over there now?" I asked and leaned forward a little. Yeah, the pounding was gonna get worse.

"She should be. Funny she didn't come outside when all the ruckus happened."

"I think I know why. You got a phone?"

"In the living room."

I stood, weaved for a second then found my footing. Dan helped me to the phone and I called to see if Pat was around. The dispatcher said he was out but if I needed him he could contact him. I told him to do that and where I was at then hung up.

CHAPTER 8

Pat came to where I was first. Once my statement given we walked over to the boarding house, and went in. It was Sally Morris that lay behind the sofa. Dan identified her, her head bashed in. Pat walked over and wrapped his hanky around the receiver of the phone and with a pen dialed the Station. The talk was short and he hung up, gave me a look and then went out onto the porch to wait for the lab boys to get here along with Ross.

I grinned and made a round of the room, most of the furniture second hand stuff, the chairs worn, the cushions almost thread bare. I mounted the stairs and walked up to the single hall that stretched the length of the house. I used a hanky to open the doors. Only two were in use, the others showed a thin film of dust on the furniture. I checked Jenny's room first, her clothes and other sundries still around.

Nothing turned up there, just the usual woman things, the dresser top covered in perfume bottles. I shivered and remembered a time when I had trailed a bail jumper to a whorehouse and got in a fight with him in his girlfriend's room, the woman finding out I would tap a woman out just as quick as a man. In the end I nailed him, but not before we almost tore the room up, the gal having a crap load of perfume also. Most of the bottles shattered in the fight and the both of us smelled to high heaven.

I went to the old woman's room next. The only furniture in her room being a bed, a rocker with a rubber donut in the seat and a dresser, two drawers holding old woman undies and her closet a couple of dresses. On the top shelf of the closet, way back in the corner I felt a photo album. I pulled it down and saw that it had been handled a lot, no dust on the covers. I flipped it open, the past coming alive in the clippings and pictures inside it.

The old woman's name was Willamina Groves, Willie for short. She had been quite a howler in her day. Pictures of her in a flapper's dress, one leg bare to the hip, a man she had the leg thrown over held a glass of booze and grinned like an idiot. There were other pictures of speakeasies, some with her sitting on men's laps, others posed beside cars with a bottle in her hand.

As I looked farther, certain men I recognized. One was of Carl Dunlop who ran the rackets when Vinnie Aldo was boss of the city. Another was of her and Gino Pascottie, the head of Aldo's bootlegging business. There were others, most of them locals. One stood out though, a fellow tall and handsome, his name scribbled on the back in faded ink along with two others. I grinned and pulled the picture lose, shoved it in my pocket and closed the book just as Pat came through the door.

"Find anything?" He nodded at the book in my hands and I handed it to him.

"The old woman's name is Willie Groves," I said as he flipped through the book. "From the looks of it she was quite a heller."

"Looks like it." He held the book out to me, the pages turned to a clipping, Willie being led out of a courthouse in handcuffs, trying to hide her face from the flashbulbs. The clipping was over thirty years old, Willie having been tried and sentenced to eighteen months in the women's penitentiary for assaulting one Frankie Russo, son of Samuel Russo, a Capo here in the city. Seems they got into a fight and Willie took his sap away from him and beat the hell out of him with it. I handed the book back to him and he closed it, tucked it under his arm and walked out of the room and back downstairs. We walked over to Ross who was knelt beside the body, his hands turned the head back and forth, checked the wound and then stood and stripped the rubber gloves from his hands.

"She's been dead a couple of hours. Somebody whacked her good." He shook his head and wadded the rubber gloves up and put them in his pocket.

"Tell me about it." I rubbed the back of my head and flinched.

"Pat tells me an old woman did this?" Ross nodded at the body. "She must have been a strong woman in the circus because it took a lot of strength to crack her skull."

"Or a lead filled sap." I grunted.

"That too." Ross answered. "Only your skull was too thick."

"Funny, very funny." Ross and Pat laughed and I shook my head and left them to finish up, I had a photo to show somebody.

***

Frank Lombardo has a social club on Olive Street, an old tailor's shop that he had bought and renovated a couple of years back. Frank's Gym is the front name for it, the first floor holding all the sundries of a training Gym for up and coming boxers, a ring in the center and a few hopefuls doing their thing. When I walked in, a few of his boys gave me the eye, wondering what the hell I was up to, the shock kept them frozen in place. I waved at them and went to the stairs leading up to the second floor. This is where Frank has his offices, well, one office, the room partitioned off, a reception area entered first, and a couple of hoods inside either reading or flipping through one of those Tijuana Bibles, a Mexican smut magazine.

By his office door sat a desk and behind that desk sat a knockout of a brunette, her hair shoulder length and cut in a Betty Paige style her eyes a deep blue under long lashes that she knew how to flutter at a guy and a set of lips that begged to be kissed. I closed the door and the two goons watched as I walked up to the desk, both not believing I was here. The woman looked up at me and smiled, the smile sexy no matter how you looked at it and asked, "Can I help you?"

For a guy like me if I was single, that would be a loaded question but so it goes if you know what I mean and I sat down on the edge of her desk and tipped my hat back, one eye on the goons and the other on her cleavage.

"Frank in?" When I asked the question, the two goons stood, hands going into their jackets and both of them facing me. My hand dipped under my jacket and I winked at her, the smile on her lips going wider, her finger on the intercom button. It was then that the door to Lombardo's office swung open. Frank stepped into the doorway and chuckled.

"Max Black, to what do I owe this pleasure?" He may have had a smile on his face but his eyes were hard and cold. I slid off the desk and walked around toward him, glanced down and smiled. The dame had a piece in her lap, a .357, her hand on the trigger.

"I came to talk Frank, just talk, no funny stuff." His smile widened and he nodded, stepped aside and motioned me into his office. His goons started to follow and he waved them off, the two hesitated then nodded and sat back down. He closed the door and walked over to his desk, waved a hand at one of the seats in front of the desk and then sat down himself.

His office was nice, dark wood paneling, deep pile carpet and bookshelves lined with books, classics. Probably first editions. The desk he sat behind was big, made of walnut and polished to a soft shine. He opened a humidor and took out a cigar, pushed the humidor toward me and I took one for myself. He clipped the end and lit up, me nipping the end with my teeth and taking the light he offered. He leaned back in his chair and studied me for a minute, his eyes still hard and his smile cold.

"So what the hell you want Black?" He spit the words out like they were something nasty. I grinned around the cigar, pulled my jacket open and dipped into the inside pocket and clipped the picture between two fingers. I leaned forward and tossed it on his desk, the picture slid across the polished surface and stopped in front of him. Lombardo picked it up and looked it over, the cigar in his mouth going from one side to the other. He grunted and tossed the picture back on his desk and looked back at me.

"Recognize anyone in the photo?" I asked the question and watched him. His eyes still cold as he grunted again and took the cigar out of his mouth. "If you don't, there's a name on the back."

"Yeah, a couple of people, where did you get it?" Lombardo had leaned forward also, his stare locked with mine.

"From the woman in the picture. I found it in her room." He picked up the picture again and looked it over, shook his head and flicked the edge of it with one finger.

"You mean Willie Groves is still alive?" He spoke her name like it was a poison. I nodded and he leaned back and said, "Hell, I thought she bought it in prison. She had a big mouth and liked to shoot it off too much. She was a wild one, you give her any shit and she would crack your skull with a sap she had made. She was good with it. Either she would crack your skull wide open or give you one hell of a headache, depended on how she felt at the time."

"I can attest to that." I rubbed the back of my head which was still sore but touchable.

"Yeah, she was a wild one." Lombardo tossed the picture back on his desk and shrugged. "Why come to me about her? If she's still around I don't know where the hell she is."

"I could care less about her." I leaned forward and tapped the picture. "Unless I ran across her again, then I'd like to give her a little back she gave to me. I…"

"You would do that to and old lady," Lombardo cut in a wicked grin on his face.

"I a heartbeat. No I want to know about this guy." I tapped the man sitting down, Willie's leg tossed over his lap and a fair amount of skin showing. Lombardo chuckled and puffed his cigar for a moment. I leaned back and waited. He gave out a long sigh and leaned forward again, tapped ash off in a crystal ashtray and scooted it toward me.

"I suppose you're not gonna leave till I tell you?"

I shrugged and said, "Unless you have me thrown out and that could get messy."

"The guy in the photo is Wilber Farnworth."

"The man who the diamonds was stolen from?"

"Yeah, he used to run with us back in the day, '31 or '32 it was. He liked being around us tough guys and we liked having him around because he would pay for the booze and, if we got busted, his old man would bail us all out of jail. Didn't last long though. His old man shipped him back east, sent him to a private school. From there he went to Yale I think it was. When his old man kicked off, they had to hunt him down, found him in a whorehouse and hauled his ass back to take over the business."

"He ever do you any favors after that?"

"Nope. Oh, he contacted me a time or two while I made my climb up the ladder, but it was more or less a social thing. He stopped a few years back, told me the last time we talked he was being watched and he didn't want to cause me to get involved in it. It was the last I heard from him."

"Who was watching him, the Feds?"

Frank leaned back again, rolled the cigar between his fingers and smiled.

"Seems his late wife had an accident, one that was a little suspicious. They were also checking out his taxes."

I knew what he was talking about now. Farnworth had been accused of whacking his wife, the woman older than him and richer. Of course money talks and a fellow by the name of Banks confessed to the murder a few days before they were going to arrest Farnworth. He got the chair and Farnworth had the VD, well, had it already but never knew it. The disease was already rotting his brain and he had an accident, fell down a flight of stairs in his home, separated his spine and had to be pushed around now. I wonder if Jenny knew about his little ailment. As to the tax investigation, that was still ongoing.

Lombardo rolled the cigar in his fingers again and looked at me over the top of it, his eyes waiting for me to say something again and instead I stood.

"Thanks Frank." I leaned over and extended my hand, his eyes narrowing a moment and then he stood and shook it. I started toward the door and he called out to me to wait. He flipped the intercom switch and told the girl out front to come into his office.

"It might not be so good an idea if you left by the front entrance," he said, the wicked smile coming back, "too many of my boys would like to have a piece of you and I want that pleasure all to myself someday."

The girl out at the desk stepped into his office. She was as lovely standing as she was sitting, more so with the tight skirt that accented every curve like a second skin.

"Linda, take Mr. Black out the back way. I'd hate to

see his early demise here in my social club."

I gave him a 'you wish' look as she hooked her arm around mine and led me to the back of his office, opened a door and led me down a flight of stairs that emptied onto a back lot. The stairway was tight and she walked beside me as we went down, her hip rubbed mine all the way down. At the bottom, she opened the door and I stepped out, my hand under my coat and a big smile on her face.

"You always this jumpy?" Her voice was sensual when she spoke, the jut of her breasts pushed against the blouse she wore and little nubs highlighted them.

"Where Lombardo is concerned, always."

"I'd say he respects you. He could of let you leave the way you came in."

"Yeah, he could have, but then he wouldn't have the pleasure of trying to off me first."

"Maybe I'll see you around before that happens?"

"I doubt it."

"Oh, you never know, I can turn up it the damnedest of places." She smiled a wicked smile and batted her eyelashes at me then turned and closed the door. I let out a low whistle and cut across the back lot, made a wide path around the block the social club was on and went to my car. The sun was slipping down behind the buildings to the west and the air had a late chill in it. I opened the car door and looked in the back, the seat empty so I crawled in.

I was about to crank over the old girl when the passenger door was yanked open, a small caliber automatic shoved in and pointed at my head. A head in a short brimmed fedora followed it and the tweed suit the face wore slid into the seat. The face behind the pistol grinned and motioned to the key in the ignition. The face was G.

"Start it up," was all G said. I could have tried to take the peashooter away from him but that would mean noise and possibly a bullet hole somewhere in the car or me. Besides, I was curious what Mr. G. wanted.

CHAPTER 9

We drove out east of town on Kearney Street, to a motel that sat out in the country just before the city picked up. Lot of farmland out this way, hay fields and pastures. The motel was a small place, six stone cottages lined the lot. Mr. G had me pull to a stop in front of one, scooted over and nudged me with the piece. I opened the door and got out, G's pistola never leaving my right side kidney.

"Number three, straight ahead." He poked me with the pistol again so I started forward. In my mind I thought about doing the stumble and spin trick, act like I tripped and then do a quick spin, my arm coming up to connect with his gun hand and hope I could knock his aim off but I kept going. I wanted to know what he was up to and maybe get a chance to tell it. I stopped at the door and he poked me again and said to open it. I turned the door knob and, with the pistola in my back stepped in.

"Walk to the middle of the room and keep your hands up." I walked, stopped in the middle of the room, hands up as he closed the door.

"Turn," he said. I did and he stepped in front of me, his

hand reaching for my pistola and sliding it out of its home. He looked it over and smiled, hefted it and felt its weight.

"You yanks, you always think bigger is better." He tossed my pistola on the bed and stepped beside me, his piece touching my side again as he reached over and pulled a chair out from the table directly behind us.

"Sit." He nudged me with the piece and I complied. "Hands behind your back please."

I reached back and felt a set of handcuffs, one set for each hand clamped around my wrists and the other end to the chair. Once done he stepped back around and smiled.

"I must say old man," he said as he pulled the other chair around and sat in front of me. "You are a persistent lot and lucky. Never have I seen a man have more luck than you do."

"Thanks." I let a slight grin cross my face and G chuckled. "So what now?"

"A few questions."

"And then?" He smiled at me, the gun in his hand bobbed up and down twice and then leveled on my belly. The smile he had on his face was one that told me then what. I smiled back and G grunted.

"First, I would like to know if you have any idea where Miss Stacks is."

"Not a clue. Last time I saw her she was hauling ass away from a boarding house with a dead woman in it and an old woman beside her in the car. Check the Toad, she works there."

"I'll do that, and I see you've met Willie. She is a feisty one that old gal."

"Yeah, she thumped my head with a sap to get away."

"With Jenny."

I nodded.

"Then she must know." He rubbed his chin and half closed his eyes, the gears turned in his mind for a few minutes and then he looked at me, the smile on his face suddenly cold.

"And what do you know?" his voice was low and threatening, the pistol raised an inch toward my chest.

"I know you are after the diamonds, mostly because of the reward."

"What makes you think that?"

I grinned and said, "A fellow like you? You have an expensive lifestyle, one that requires a lot of money to keep up appearances. I'd say that money is now almost gone. The Big Boys have cheated you and you are hoping on a double payoff."

He laughed, tossed his head back and let her rip. When he was done he looked at me and shrugged.

"Well, it didn't start out that way. I learned about the diamonds from Farnworth. He contacted me with a plan to have the diamonds stolen and once the money from the insurance claim was paid, I was to get a small percentage of it plus the diamonds to fence. But Jenny came along with her oiled boyfriend and beat me to it. I'll have to say he is good with a safe. Farnworth called me after it happened, told me he would pay a reward of five hundred thousand to anyone who could retrieve them for him."

"Anyone huh?"

"Sad to say yes. It was leaked to the unsavory side of the populace. Farnworth figured what better than thieves to gain back what he had lost."

"So in other words, Jerry and Jenny tossed a wrench in your master scheme?"

"So it would seem." G stood, his eyes locked with mine and a somber look came on his face, the pistola in his hand tapped his lower lip. "Now, what to do with you?"

He stood and I gave a little shrug and smiled at him, my teeth showing through my lips.

"You know, for a master planner, you sure are a stupid son of a bitch."

"How so?"

"You left my feet free." It was fast. One minute I was seated and the next I was on my feet, the two feet between us suddenly inches and then my head slammed into his chest and I kept pushing. We hit the door hard, the pistola in his hand going off once then fell from his hand to clatter on the floor. He wasn't down and out though. He was a strong little guy. His hands grabbed my shoulders and he shoved me back. The chair and me hit the floor and the chair, a second hand job shattered my hands free.

I jumped to my feet just as he grabbed the pistola, my right hand still hooked to part of the chair back. I gripped it in my hand and swung as I stepped to the left, his piece going off and the slug burning a path across my coat. The chair back came up and slammed into his side. He folded but fired again. This time he got lucky and the slug creased my temple as I rammed him again, both of us going through the door and out into the lot. Then the lights dimmed and the world fell in on me.

**

The smelling salts brought me out of it.

I groaned and then opened my eyes, blurry but clearing so I closed them again and then opened them back up. The face of an old man looked down at me. He smiled and then waved the smelling salts under my nose again. This time I jerked and knocked his hand away.

"Reflexes normal." He chuckled and set the salts on the bedside table. "You was lucky, a hair's breadth more and you would be singin' with the angels or would it be dancin' with the devil? Which would it be?

"Probably the latter," I said and tried to sit up. My head swan and I let out a moan and the old man pushed me back. This keeps up and I might get addlebrained.

"Take it easy buddy, try not to rush it."

"My car..."

"Is fine," he said. "The other guy tried to take off in it and I took a shot at him, missed but he took off on foot like a bat out of hell. I also got your piece. Damned fine pistol there."

"Thanks." I eased myself up and he helped, this time my head didn't swim but throbbed.

"Names Doc Lyons. I own this place, sort of a retirement home so to speak."

I nodded and tried to stand, the room tilting so I sat back down. Doc shook his head and stood, walked over to the bathroom and took a bottle of aspirin off the shelf and brought three to me. I popped them in my mouth and swallowed, the old man's eyes sparkling. He had to be close to seventy, his hair white and very little of that left. He had a grizzled face, white stubble covered his jaws and chin and he wore a pair of wire rimmed glasses, the lenses thick and magnified his eyes.

"What the hell was you two fightin' about?" He sat down on the edge of the bed and I grunted. Then I remembered the cuffs, looked at my wrists and they were bare. Doc chuckled.

"Lookin' for those?" He chuckled and pointed at the nightstand. "Cops ain't the only ones who have keys to those. Was he a cop?"

"No, a hood." I tried to stand again and this time made it.

"Figured as much." Doc said. "He had that look about him."

"Yeah, thanks." I took a couple of steps, my legs a little rubbery but holding. I made it to the door and stopped, turned and gave him a look. Doc grinned and shook his head.

"Nope, didn't call the cops. Them suckers would have been here most of the night and I got things they don't need to see." He winked and I smiled. The things he didn't want them to see were probably out back. A copper pot and tubing plus maybe a few jars of that wondrous elixir known as moonshine. I laughed and headed out the door.

***

The pounding in my head eased up a bit as I parked in the lot across from my office and headed down to Kelso's. Kelso's was a little livelier than the last time I was here. Regulars and a few new faces crowded the bar. The juke was playing big band to rock and roll and people were dancing in a small open area. Fisk was at his usual spot, slightly turned, watching the dancers and the bar. When I walked in a couple of fellows were getting loud at the bar. One was a young punk, leather jacket, pompadour haircut, motorcycle boots and a cigarette hung from the corner of his mouth.

The other guy was older, wrinkled suit, scuffed shoes and a hat that was in need of a good cleaning. They were talking about the war, not the last one but the Korean one going on now. I figured it was about the draft, the two getting loud for a few minutes then settling down. I walked up to Fisk's booth and slid in, his eyes cut toward me and after a few minutes, he slid around and faced me.

"Trouble?" I asked the question and Fisk shrugged, picked up the beer in front of him and drank some of it before he spoke.

"Probably will be," he answered. "Kids have got no respect for the older generation anymore. Looks like you've had some trouble yourself?"

"Nothing I can't handle."

"So what's on your mind?"

I told him about G and the diamonds. Fisk shook his head and a small smile crossed his face. Then I told him what I suspected Stills was up to.

"Yeah, I've heard rumbles that he might be on his way out. Seems that two of his biggest supporters pulled out on him."

"Why?"

"Well, you've heard the old saying about scratching one's back?"

I nodded.

"Remember the Parker trial?"

"Yeah, the kid who robbed the mom and pop store and almost beat the old man to death?"

"Uh-huh. Seems this supporter was kin to the kid, wanted Stills to let him off easy. Instead of felonious assault, he wanted Stills to charge the kid with misdemeanor assault and give him probation. Stills refused. Mostly because the kid had been jailed three times before on assault charges and got off and to let him walk wouldn't look good with the press. The paper even hinted that the kid would probably get off with a slap on the wrist since he had relatives in high places. If he did, maybe the public should consider if they wanted a D.A. who catered to high society or the law. Stills threw the book at the kid after that was printed and his biggest contributors pulled out on him with maybe a few lesser supporters waiting in the wings to see what was gonna happen."

"So it is about the election?" Fisk nodded at me and laced his fingers together and leaned back. I chuckled and sat back also.

"What?" Fisk leaned forward again and stared at me. "Something you know that I don't?"

I smirked and nodded, another thought crossed my mind as I said, "You know about the reward for the return of the diamonds?"

"Yeah, five hundred g's."

"Think about it, if Stills could nab the diamonds before the others could…"

"Wait, what others."

I gave him a shocked look and leaned on the table toward him, his face stony as I told him about Jenny and

Jerry who were looking for the same payoff.

"Jenny and Jerry are after the diamonds along with this Mr. G." Fisk shook his head.

"Well, it's a little more complicated than that with them. I suspect they want the diamonds *and* the revenue from the casino. I'd say that is what the map is about. I just need to get to the diamonds before they get delivered or when they are delivered."

"You got the map?"

"No, but I drew a copy of it for Pat before I saw the world from a jail cell but that doesn't mean I don't remember it." I took a napkin from the holder and a pen from my pocket and sketched it out on the napkin. Fisk's eyes narrowed a couple of times and when I was finished, I scooted it over toward him. He eyed it for a few minutes and then looked up at me, a big grin on his face.

"This," he said tapping the building that had been missing from the original map, "is the casino, right?"

"Yeah."

"So the circles with x's in them are pickup points and I know exactly what businesses they are."

He tapped the first circle and said, "This one is a cleaners, across the street from Mama Jeans, there's a wire service on the second floor. I hear they pick up a lot of green from it, almost as much as the casino makes. The second one is a loan shark business, not a lot of money comes out of there but the Big Boys get their cut no matter what. This building, with the check, this is the drop off point, the money handed off and then one of the Chicago men picks it up. If there is anything to deliver he leaves it there."

"How come Lombardo's men don't make the drive to Chi?"

Fisk chuckled and said, "The drive is supposed to be a straight through, no stops unless it is for gas. Lombardo's last man decided it was a bunch of bullshit and stopped at a diner on the way. While he was there the diner got robbed and guess what? The robbers had already robbed a business and their car was hot so they took Lombardo's driver's car."

I made a face and let out a low whistle. No doubt the driver was either in a shallow grave somewhere along the river or he was beat half to death and then dumped in front of some hospital. I went back to the map and tapped the check-marked building.

"And this building is?"

"Myer's Second Hand Shop."

"Pinky Myers?"

"That's the one."

I leaned back and grunted. Pinky Myers was a fixture around this city, his business having been in one place or the other over the years. Back during Prohibition, he ran a speakeasy from the basement of one of his stores, palms greased to keep John Law off his back.

When booze became legal, he moved to the fencing business and I don't mean barbed wire. Times were changing though and greasing John Law's hand didn't cut it anymore. Pinky was busted in a sting and spent seven years in the state hotel. When he got out he vowed he was going straight, promised he would be a model citizen. Yeah right.

This time though he had the Big Boys covering him, their head of lettuce bigger and greener.

"So when do these pickups happen?" I asked.

"Once a month. The revenue is picked up and taken to Myers. Myers and his boys count and bundle up what is left after the others take their cut and the rest is boxed up and then shipped out. The driver usually leaves with a hundred to a hundred fifty thousand."

"And he delivers the diamonds?"

"Probably, but I doubt the boys from Chi know anything about them. I mean, do you think someone in the family would let those babies get away if they knew about them? No, I figure Lombardo has made arrangements with the pickup man to receive the rocks along the way, paying him a little bonus to keep his mouth shut."

"So when is the next pickup?"

"This Friday."

That gave me four days. I stood and held out my hand, Fisk shaking and the money passing. I turned to walk toward the front door and the kid in the leather coat came backpedaling at me, his hands and arms making circles in the air as he tried to get his balance. I braced myself as he slammed into me, looped an arm around his neck and popped him on the side of the head. He grunted and went slack but not out. I gave Kelso a salute and pulled the kid along with me, his feet pushing him part of the way, the rest I dragged along. I figured he had been lucky I had a hold of him. The old guy looked pissed enough to make him into a chopped steak. I'd drop him on the sidewalk, Kelso would have tossed him in the garbage.

CHAPTER 10

I had four days to get ready. Four days to find out what route the delivery man was taking and then set up a sting of my own. I needed the diamonds for that though so I called an old friend of mine at the highway patrol department, a fellow I had gotten out of a jam when his wife had gotten in over her head at the dice table when Russo ran the casino.

He met me at a gas station on 65 highway just outside of Fair Grove to the north of Springfield. He told me there were a couple of routes that were possible. One to the northeast, mostly back roads skirting the city. Another to the southwest, more of a direct route but still skirting the city. I asked him why they hadn't nailed the guy yet and he told me there were only two of them to patrol from here to Sedalia, you figure it out? He said the southwest route was quicker, the roads not as good but if anyone got after him he has a lot of back roads he could lose the law on.

I thanked him and he asked why all the curiosity. I told him it was complicated and mostly personal. He laughed, shook my hand and told me to be careful.

***

I had a plan and Shelly was gonna be a part of it. No shooting it out with the bad guys unless we had to but I would need her help. When I got back to the office I sat her down and told her what I wanted to do. She nodded a couple of times then patted the .357 under her arm and asked when we started. I told her to hold onto her garters. I had a few other things to take care of in the next four days.

First, I staked out Myer's second hand store. A lot of fancy suits and hats went in and out of the back door of the place. Some of them I knew but there were about half that were new. Then I got a break. Willie came and visited Myers, stayed a couple of hours and then left. I fired up my old heap and tailed her and hoped she would lead me to Jenny and Jerry.

She drove to Water Street and turned south on a side street. The car she drove a 32 Ford, fenders banged up and one back glass busted out and replaced with cardboard. She drove down the street, then turned into a service alley, her car stopping and the old woman got out and walked up to a steel door.

I drove on past the alley, parked on the shoulder of the side street and crawled out, checked my .45 to see if one was in the chamber and headed back to the service alley. The car was gone, either she hadn't stayed very long or someone from inside had come out and moved it. I walked down the alley, the only door visible the one she had entered. I looked the door over. Solid steel, no handle on the outside or keyhole either. I shrugged and knocked. There was the sound of a bolt being pulled back and a lever pulled up.

The door opened, the guy on the other side started to say something then he froze, his eyes bugged and he shoved his hand under his jacket. I grabbed his shirt front with my left hand before his hand could come out from under the jacket, jerked him forward and out the doorway then spun him around, my right hand swung up and the muzzle of my pistol connected with his jaw, the hit solid. His jaw snapped shut and his eyes rolled back as I let him drop to the cobblestone alley.

I dug the .38 out from under his coat and slipped it into my jacket pocket then entered the doorway and closed the door behind me. There was a short hallway ahead of me, no doors just hallway. The end of it spilt out onto a raised platform, crates and old furniture stacked around on it. I weaved my way around the stuff and saw a ramp that led down to the floor. I went to it and down, the shadows dark in places, naked light bulbs glowed in certain spots under the platform lighting the floor for a few feet the ending in solid darkness.

The floor was flat for probably five or six feet then is started to slope up. Light showed at the top of the slope. Three sets of doors were there, one of them open. The light spilled out from them a few feet then faded into the darkness. I walked up the slope close to the wall, my eyes used to the darkness after a few minutes. The room was big and empty, carpet runners along the wall and in between large open spots ran all the way to the upper level. Dimly I could see a balcony and I knew where I was at. The old Hamilton Theater, a Vaudeville house back when it first opened, then a movie house till about 1946 then it closed. At the top I eased along until I came to the open door, some light coming from a couple of electric bulbs.

I crouched and peeked through the doorway into what had once been the lobby. The room had a dirty and threadbare carpet on it, a counter stood to my left and an old popcorn machine stood on the counter, the inside a little green from mold where they hadn't gotten the butter cleaned out of it good. Candy racks lined the walls behind the counter, some candy boxes still stacked on the racks, dust and cobwebs clung to them. One of the doors was boarded over, specks of light showing where the boards didn't fit together good, the other door was uncovered, the glass soaped over, a few cracks in it from either the elements or someone trying to bust it out. Along the south wall was a staircase, a dim light at the top. If I played it right I might catch them with their pants down, if not, then I might be screwed if I couldn't find a way out.

I listened for a few minutes, nothing moved in the area past the door so I stepped out, still crouched and was glad I did. A goon swung a club where my head should have been, the club cut nothing but air and my fist found his cajones, his eyes bugged and he screamed, doubled over as he fell to the floor gagging and pawing his crotch.

I gave him a kick to the head as my hand went under my coat and grabbed the butt of my .45, a door slammed open at the top of a staircase. Other doors slammed open behind me and men came barreling out. I took out four of them before they took me down. I saw stars and then the world went black, the woman at the top of the stairs cackled as I drifted toward darkness.

***

I opened my eyes just enough to see what was going on in the room around me. They had me in a chair, one of those metal jobs you see down in the interrogation room of the Station. My hands were tied behind me, the rope looped around my chest and then tied off in the back. Two hoods lounged on an old table, one of them smoked while the other played with my .45. I could hear other voices in the room, muted but there. The room was shadowed. A couple of bulbs giving off a dirty light hung down from the ceiling by a single wire. The floor was dusty and I could see tracks and drag marks where they had hauled me in and tied me to the chair. Bits and pieces of junk sat in the shadows, tables and other stuff stacked in piles around the walls.

"Wakey, wakey asshole." It was Willie, her voice raspy from years of cigarettes, whiskey or both. "I seen you open your eyes and look the place over."

I opened my eyes and looked up at her and grinned, her face even with mine. Her face retained none of the beauty it once had. The whiskey, cigarettes and hard living had lined her face deeply. Her skin looked like old leather, dark and spotted, her lips thin and pulled back tight across her mouth, her three yellowed teeth showing in the thin line her lips made. Her eyes were dark slits in her face and her hair was gray and looked like old, weathered straw pulled back in a tight bun on the back of her head.

"Let me crack his head, just enough that he'll be real cooperative." They should have tied my legs. When she looked back at me and grinned I swept one foot out. Willie's eyes widened and she yelped. One foot came out from under her and she sat down hard. I drew back my foot for a kick at her face and someone behind me thumped me on the head. The room spun for a second and then stopped, Willie on her feet and ready to come at me.

"Get her out of here," a voice growled as the two hoods who lounged on the table jumped down, grabbed her and hauled her ass out of the room. Willie screamed she was gonna split my head like a melon. I looked back to where the voice had come from, the cherry end of a cigarette glowed in the shadows and then he stepped forward.

Jerry Ventura had a butt in his mouth and a big smile held it there. He was dressed in a gray suit, an expensive three piece job with collared vest and a gold watch chain draped across the front. One thumb hung from one pocket of the vest, his free hand came up and pushed his dark gray fedora back a little. His face was long and a little pointed, his eyes hooded behind narrowed lids as he walked into the light. He reminded me of a ferret.

"You should thank me. She wanted to split your skull

before you woke up." The cigarette bobbed between Jerry's lips and his smile grew bigger.

"I'll make a mental note. Where's your partner?" I asked the question and he shrugged.

"At work."

"Casing the joint huh? Making sure that when the money goes out there's enough to fool with."

"Something like that." He took the cigarette out and flicked ash on the floor as he stepped back even with a support and leaned on it. I'd been working my hands all the while we had been talking, the sweat and some blood making my skin slick. The ropes slipped a little at a time.

"Which one of you killed the kid?" I asked this and his face seemed to darken a little. Jerry drew hard on the cigarette, the cherry almost burned down to his fingers before he stopped. He blew the smoke out at me in a hard stream, his lips tight across his teeth as he spoke.

"It had to be done." His lips barely moved and even though I couldn't see his eyes I could tell they were drilling into me. "He should have taken the offer. Kept his mouth shut and he would've had money to burn."

"You didn't answer my question?" I drilled his eyes back and he grunted, dropped the cigarette on the floor and ground it out with his shoe so I asked, "How much you offer him?"

"Three percent of the take."

"Of how much?"

"Probably seventy, eighty thousand."

"Is that after Lombardo takes his cut plus skims a little for his own bank account?"

"What's that supposed to mean?"

"Come on Jerry, you know how it works. Lombardo takes his cut *before* the money is bagged up and taken out of the casino. He also skims a little off the top for his personal use. I'd say there probably isn't any more than forty thousand left when the money arrives at the pickup point. Plus the payoffs, probably will leave you with twenty, thirty thousand."

"So? Twenty, thirty thousand is a lot of bread. A fellow can live pretty comfortable on that kind of green. Besides, from what I've heard there is a lot more than that comes out of the casino."

"Even so, how long you figure to live once you heist the money?"

He laughed then said, "Oh, we got it all figured out shamus. We won't be on the run in this country for very long. Jenny has a friend down in Florida who can get us on a boat to Cuba. We plan on buying a villa there and maybe have a little face work done. We'll have plenty left to live pretty comfortable. Along with the diamonds, well…"

"Sounds like a plan unless someone rats you out." I gave him a wicked grin. "The Big Boys have a lot of connections down there. Hell, they own some of the casinos in Havana. Better do a complete face lift if you're gonna go there because someone will recognize you and then…bang." I said the last word soft and loud. Jerry bounded off the pole and started to take a step toward me then stopped.

"Bullshit!"

I shrugged and one of the loops around my wrist slipped off I had been working on.

"You two plan on doing this alone?" Another loop slipped free and I relaxed but held onto the rope to keep it from loosening around my chest.

"We got a confidant. Jenny has been working on him since she went to work there."

"You gonna pay him a percentage too?"

Jerry shook his head and came over in front of me, leaned down and chuckled in my face.

"So he thinks."

"What about Willie, she in on this?"

"She thinks she is. Once she takes care of you then I'll

take care of her and her two goons. So long shamus. If I
was you I'd piss her off so she'll crack your head and
you'll go quickly."

He came over and pinched my cheek hard, slapped it
and laughed. I laughed back and my hands came out, my
thumbs clamped on his eyes and pushed. He screamed as I
came up out of the chair, shoved him back and followed
him as he grabbed at my arms and staggered backward. I
slammed him into one of the hoods by the table, both guys
just starting to react. I let go and both of them fell
backwards in a heap. The hood with my .45 leveled it at
me. He got off one shot, the slug hissed over my head and
hit the other hood, who came up off the floor from under
Jerry.

Before he could aim again I was on him. My head hit
him dead center in the stomach, the air slammed out of him
and my .45 knocked from his hand. He was on his back,
gasping and grabbing under his coat. I gave him a nasty
smile and gripped the .38 in my jacket pocket and fired
twice. The bullets ripped holes in my jacket and also in his
throat. He gasped again, gurgled, arched his back and
grabbed his throat then flattened out, coughed some blood,
then died. Feet were pounding on the floor outside so I
bent, picked up my .45 and started to step out the door.
Then I saw the trench gun, a sawed off Winchester 12
gauge propped by the door.

I smiled and picked it up, pumped a shell into the
chamber and fired at the door. A few screams and dropping
bodies sounded on the other side. I kicked the door open
and stepped out onto the landing, one hood at the head of
the steps breathing his last as he tried to stop his guts from
leaking out. Another hood was to my right, his face a
twisted mask as he aimed his piece. I pulled the trigger and
his head decorated the wall behind him.

I have to hand it to Winchester, they make a fine
firearm. Two more went down as they barreled up the steps

toward me before they decided to quit. Willie's voice was loud as she cussed them and called them pussies and to get the hell out of her way. She yelled up at me and told me she was coming, she had a surprise and I heard the bolt of a Chicago typewriter slam back.

She would probably open up before she hit the top two steps so I lay down on the floor and waited. Her head came into view first, then the snout of the chatter box. I aimed and fired at the top half of her head as it came into view, the double 00 buck slammed into her forehead, took the top off and pitched her back down the steps. I jacked another shell in the trench gun and waited, nobody else came into view so I stood, crouched down and went over to the steps.

The rest of Jerry's crew had bolted. Only Willie lay at the bottom, the top of her head completely gone, her eyes in their sockets glared up at me.

CHAPTER 11

Jerry was gone when I went back into the room, a door back in the shadows led to a staircase and then down to the bottom floor. A side door led to the street I was parked on, the door still open. My trench coat lay on a chair beside the table so I grabbed it up and headed toward the door, the stairway not having been used in a while, scuff marks in the dust showed on the stair steps.

Outside I looked around, tried to spot Jerry. If he had of been able to see to get to the street I hadn't done my job but he was nowhere in sight. Evidently I hadn't done my job. I walked back to my car, ears and eyes open in case he had found a hiding place. He hadn't. I checked my car out good also, aimed the trench gun at the window of the car as I opened the front door and looked the insides over. He wasn't there.

I crawled in, fired the old gal up and drove to the end of the street, turned west and came out on Campbell Street, watching the sidewalks and alleys in case Jerry had made it this far. On the corner of Campbell and McDaniel there was a drugstore so I pulled into the curb and parked. The place was small, a short lunch counter on the north side, six or seven stools, a small soda fountain and a grill, the menu consisting mostly of sandwiches.

At the end of the counter sat a kid, dressed in white, perched on a stool and reading a paperback. A glass cased counter lined the south side. Shelves behind the counter filled with the usual sundries drugstores carried. The glass case was filled with Knickknacks, junk that most people looked at but never bought. On the east wall was an open phone so I dug a few dimes out and dialed Shelly first.

"Hey kitten, what's up?" There was a pause for a moment and then she spoke, her tone of voice on the hard side.

"Where you been?" I took in a deep breath and let it out slow before I answered.

"I had a little dustup. Nothing to worry about."

"I know the kind of dustups you get into buddy." Her voice was low. "And they usually *are* something to worry about."

"You heard from Pat?" I changed the subject and she paused and mumbled something under her breath before she spoke.

"He's called once. I told him when you called I would have you get hold of him."

"He tell you anything?"

"No just that you were to call him. Max…" She let the words drop off and I waited. "Stills was by here awhile ago. He grilled me as to where you were and I told him I didn't have a clue. He just the same as called me a liar and said he would be back, that if you called to tell you to get your ass back here. He wanted to have a word with you."

I grunted and shook my head. Now he was harassing my secretary. Not good Stills, not good at all. The guy was shoving his weight around again but doing it behind my back. Shelly sounded upset and that was the clincher for me.

"He comes back and I'm not there, you tell him to take

a hike."

"He'll be pissed."

"So let him. Don't worry kitten. You haven't heard from me yet. Tell him that."

"Okay, be careful Max, he's out for blood."

"So am I." I told her bye and hung up, shoved another dime in the phone and called the Station. Used to, before they put in the dial system, you could tell the operator to connect you directly with someone, now when you dialed the Station, the phone rang in at the switchboard and the switchboard connected you. Pat's phone rang three times before he picked it up.

"Hey buddy, you busy?"

"Not at the moment. I was a while ago. Stills was here."

"That so? He's been to see Shelly also. What's he up too?"

"That is anybody's guess but I suppose since it is an election year he is trying to make points with the masses."

"Uh-huh."

"What's that mean?"

"Nothing. Meet me here at the drugstore on Campbell and McDaniel. I have something to tell you."

I hung up while Pat was still talking into the phone. I stepped into the small bathroom by the phone, the cube just big enough for one person. I washed the blood from my hands and looked into the mirror, a couple of bruises on my chin starting to purple up. There were rope burns on my wrists from my working the ropes loose and some blood from the scrapes colored the cuffs of my shirt. I looked in the mirror and shook my head.

I felt suddenly drained. Maybe it was time to hang it up. I splashed water on my face and used paper towels to dry it and my hands. Maybe Shelly was right. I grinned and shook my head, tossed the paper towel in the trash and stepped out of the bathroom.

I went over to the lunch counter and slid onto a stool. The kid folded a page over in the paperback and tossed it on the counter as he walked toward me. He was a tall, skinny kid, thin in the face with bushy eyebrows and no lips, just thin strips that showed he had a set. His nose was flat and had a ball on the end and his eyes, blue as the sky, were magnified behind the glasses he wore. His hair was short on the sides and his ears stuck out like sails.

"Something to eat or drink?" He asked the question in a bored voice as he looked at me. I picked up a menu and scanned it, the selections sparse so I tossed it on the counter.

"A soda, a little bit of cherry flavor in it." He nodded and went over to the fountain, drew up the soda and squirted a little flavor in it, looked over his shoulder at me to see if it was enough. I nodded and he brought it over.

I pulled a straw out of the container and slid it into the glass, stirred and then sipped, nodded it was okay and he started to walk back to his seat. He slid up on the stool and picked up his paperback, opened it but looked at me instead. My picture had been in the paper a lot as of late. Andy Robinson, crime reporter for *The Leader*, carrying on a one man crusade against me. Every time I get in a dustup with some hoods, Andy writes a three column squib ranting about the vigilante judgment I am doling out. He says the Wild West is no longer in vogue and I should be chained and flogged for some of the things I do. He and Stills make a perfect fit.

The kid was about to slide off his seat and come over to where I sat when Pat walked in, slid up next to me and tipped his fedora back. He waved the kid off thinking he was coming over to see if he wanted anything and the kid made a face and planted himself back on the stool. Pat had his cop look on. His hand pulled a pack of Lucky's out of his jacket pocket and shook one loose. I waited till he had it lit and had taken a couple of drags before I looked at him.

His eyes told me he wasn't happy.

"A few bodies were found in the old Hamilton Theater. You know anything about that?" The cigarette in his mouth bobbed as he spoke, his eyes locked with mine and narrowed. I shrugged and sipped the soda in front of me, a slow smile turned up the corners of my mouth. Somebody had heard the commotion and called the law.

"Stills was in my office when the call came in. Like the good D.A. he is he went with me. Two hoods had bullet holes in them, an old woman at the foot of the stairs had the top of her head blown off from what the lab's boys said was possibly a shotgun blast. Stills said it was some of your work. I told him you didn't use a shotgun."

"I improvised. The trench gun was handy and I had only one bullet left in my pistola. She had a chatter box and I didn't think I could dodge slugs on the landing."

"Stills is pissed. He wants me to take your gun and have ballistics check the slugs in the bodies to see if they're yours."

"And they wouldn't be, but it was warranted."

"How so?"

I showed him my wrists and hands, the rope burns visible on my wrists. Pat took his hat off and tossed it on the counter, let out a sigh and shook his head.

"So why didn't you call it in?"

I shrugged again and Pat pointed a finger at me, his voice low and his eyes narrowed.

"Stills wants me to bring you in, take your .45 away from you and toss your ass in a cell."

"And is that what *you* want to do?"

"Hell no," Pat shook his head, "but you're gonna have to level with me if you want to stay out of jail."

I sipped the soda again and then pushed it back, turned toward him and slid from the stool, motioned for him to follow me as I tossed a quarter on the counter and walked toward the door. Once outside, I had him follow me to my car and told him to get in his and follow me. He gave me a questioning look but walked to his heap and slid in as I started up my old heap and pulled out, cut down a side street and then drove over to Booneville Street, pulled onto the parking lot on the corner of St. Louis and Booneville. We were on a rise, the parking lot looked down on Myer's business, the back door visible from where we sat.

"And the reason we are here is?" He cocked his head toward me and arched an eyebrow as he stepped up beside me.

I told him about the money pickups and that Myer's was the place where the loot ended up to be counted, bundled up and then shipped out. I also told him about the diamonds and what I suspected was going to go down with Jerry and Jenny. Pat let out a low whistle and watched the back door. A car pulled up and a couple of hoods got out, waltzed in the back door, stayed a few minutes and then came out and left.

"You think he is running a wire service in there also?"

"Possibly. A lot of back door activity goes on both day and night. Once a month someone from Chi comes and makes a pickup. I have it on good authority that at the end of this week the messenger will come to pick up the green and also to deliver the diamonds."

"The Farnworth rocks?" Pat's eyes widened and he looked back at Myers place.

I nodded.

"But how…" Pat let the words trail off.

"It's complicated old buddy. Let's just let it play out and then I'll fill you in."

"Yeah," he said as I started to crawl back in my car. The pop of a gunshot shattered my windshield, a slug passed so close to my ear I could hear the whine of it. Pat already had his .38 out and ducked for cover, tossing off shots at the gunman. The windshield was one of the new kind, shatters in a million spider cracks, impossible to see out of but there was no flying glass. I tossed open my door and crouched behind it, my .45 out as Pat did the same. Another shot hit my door, thumped into it and punched a dimple in the inside panel.

I raised up. Two hoods were behind a couple of parked cars, one with a rifle and the other with a revolver. The guy with the rifle leaned out a bit, his eye sighting down the barrel. I aimed and squeezed off a shot, the hood screamed and spun off the car, the rifle clattering to the ground between the cars. The other hood raised up a bit, looked over at his buddy and suddenly realized it was the wrong thing to do. Pat fired, the hood yelped and fell backward over the rail along the raised parking lot.

We both ran in a crouch toward the rail. The one I had shot groaned as he tried to sit up, the muzzle of my .45 stared him in the face. His eyes went wide and he raised his hands. Pat looked over the rail, the sidewalk empty. The hood that had fallen nowhere to be seen, only a blood spot on the sidewalk where he had landed.

I motioned with the muzzle of my pistola for the hood to get up. Pat walked around behind me and picked up the rifle. The hood had been lucky, my slug had grazed the side of his head, a nasty red whelp showed across his temple and part of his ear was missing. I'd been aiming at the middle of his forehead, he must have moved. I stepped up to him, the smile on my face nasty as I shoved my .45 under his chin and pushed hard enough for him to stand on his tip toes. His eyes went wider, bugged as I stepped in closer and walked him back to the rail.

"You owe me a windshield asshole," I hissed at him.

"Fuck you," he grunted. It's not easy talking with a .45 jammed under your chin so I eased back a bit.

"Who you working for?" He grunted again shook his head so I stomped the top of his foot, stomped it hard and ground my foot down on it at the same time shoving the muzzle of my pistola hard under his chin again.

"One last chance buddy. I get no answer this time I pull the trigger and look for them elsewhere." Sweat was rolling down his face, his eyes were still bugged as he tried to swallow but couldn't. "Who?"

I eased back on my .45 again and he finally swallowed, opened his mouth to say something and then jerked, the sound of a shot loud, his eyes blinked once then he slumped forward, the only thing that kept him on his feet was my piece under his chin. I let him fall as I stepped back and took cover behind the car. Pat had done the same and we waited. No other shot came and I peeked up over the trunk of the car, ready to jerk back down if there was another shot.

Pat and I both stood, but kept the cars between us and the street. Pat knelt to check on the hood, a bullet in his back between his shoulder blades, a red circle growing on the back of his jacket as sirens sounded down the street and filled the air.

***

Pat told me to take a hike. I started to tell him no but he grabbed me by the arm and led me across the lot to St. Louis Street.

"Take off, go up on the square and catch a cab or ride the bus, just get the hell out of here. Stills will probably show up and this will give him reason to detain you," he said to me. He looked over his shoulder and walked away.

"What about my car?"

"I'll take care of it. Just go!" He turned and walked back to the place where the body lay. I crossed the street and cut into the covered walkway between the Heers Building and the store next door. Red lights and sirens flashed down the walkway and boomed in my ears as they passed. I paused and looked back. Another car pulled up, this one a black Buick, the back door flying open and Stills getting out before the car even stopped.

I turned and hustled up to the square, a cab parked close to the Heers building, its sign off. I opened the door and crawled in, the driver looking over at me and asking where I wanted to go. I told him and also said he might wanna avoid St. Louis Street. There had been some trouble back there. He nodded and pulled his meter flag down, pulled out and took Olive Street down to Campbell then headed north toward Commercial.

"What kind of trouble was it mac?" He glanced over his shoulder at me, the same face that had taken a header over the rail at the parking lot. I shrugged, hoping my face hadn't given me away as I eased my hand under my coat and leaned forward. The hood suddenly slammed on the brakes, slamming me into the front seat which bounced me back. I drew as I hit the back seat. The driver had a .38 in his hand, a bloody hand. He thought he had me, a Cheshire cat smile on his face as he raised the weapon. He never got to fire.

My .45 roared in the close confines of the cab, two shots, all I had left in the clip. They punched holes in the back of the front seat, the hood jerking with each hit. I jumped out of the cab before the hood's foot could slip off the brake, made a beeline just as it did and opened his door. I shoved him over hard and slid in beside him as the car jerked a couple of times but didn't die.

I slammed the door and stomped the clutch, tossed the cab in gear and took off. I headed toward Commercial Street, the dead hood on the seat beside me, a look of surprise on his face which made me laugh. I pulled into the parking lot behind the Crank's Drugstore on the west side of Booneville Street, parked the cab in one of the slots and shut off the motor. Before I crawled out, I searched the hood, keeping one eye on the parking lot and the other on what I might find.

No ID but there was a matchbook from the Horned

Toad, an address and phone number written on the inside. I grinned and slipped the matchbook in my pocket, crawled out and took the keys with me to the back of the cab, opened the trunk and shook my head. The cabbie was stuffed in the trunk, a hole in his head and a shocked look on his face. I closed the trunk and walked back around to the passenger door, opened it and shoved the keys back in the ignition, closed the door and crossed the street. I pulled a cigar out and lit up as I walked up the street to the office, a smile on my face as I thought about the address and phone number in the matchbook.

CHAPTER 12

At the office I called Pat and told him about the body in the cab behind the Drugstore. He groaned and started to answer me when someone jerked the phone away from him and started yelling into it. Stills was in rare form, every other word turned the air blue. I listened and when he ran out of steam I calmly asked to talk to Pat again. I could hear Stills teeth grinding against each other as he told me I didn't need to talk to Pat on the phone. They would be there in ten minutes.

I hung up and chuckled to myself. Good old D.A. Stills thought he had me. I pulled the matchbook out of my pocket and stared at the phone number inside the cover. Shelly had already gone home so I walked out into her office and sat down at her desk, tucked the matchbook in my vest pocket and propped my feet up waiting for Stills and Pat to arrive.

While I waited, I made another phone call, this one to a buddy of mine who worked out at the casino. I asked him a few questions and he told me a lot of things, one of them being that Stills had an informant out of the casino, something I suspected from the phone number in the matchbook but had to be sure of. I asked my buddy if the informant was working tonight and he said no, hadn't been in for a couple of nights but he knew where he was. I told him to get him and bring him to my office. He said with pleasure.

Around seven in the evening, Pat and Stills came by. Stills slammed into my office, his face red and his voice loud.

"I've got you now you son of a bitch!" He almost yelled the words as he reached over and knocked my feet off the desk. "Stand up, you're under arrest."

"For what?" I placed my feet back up on the desk and grinned at him. He growled and knocked them off again.

"Murder." I gave him a nasty grin, looked at my office doorway and my buddy, Jimmy shoved a small man out into the room. He was thin and shaking, his face tight and his eyes looking from me to Stills. I chuckled as Stills' mouth worked but nothing came out. The red left his face and was replaced with a pale white. I propped my feet back up on the desk again. Stills' hands clenched tight, his body shaking a little.

"Who's this?" Pat asked the question and the skinny guy jerked his head around, his eyes narrowed and he looked back at Stills.

"Casper Pell, he's a gofer for Lombardo's boys and also an informant." I looked at Stills. Casper took a step forward, his face tight as his eyes drilled into Stills.

"You bastard," he stepped in close to Stills. "You said after I did what you wanted you'd fix it with the cops."

"I…I don't know what you're talking about," Stills stuttered.

"I think you do." I stood and stepped between them. "You're little friend here has been keeping you informed about all the goings on out at the Toad. Especially the diamonds that Lombardo is to receive this Friday."

"What do you know about the diamonds?" Pat stepped closer to the skinny man and he took a step back. Jimmy slipped in behind him and he bumped into him. His head jerked around, a snarl coming from his throat.

"Yeah, the Farnworth Diamonds," I said, "Lombardo got them somehow. The guy who picks up the money from the casino to take up north will have them. I'm sure Lombardo made a deal with him and the boys up north have no idea about it, right?"

I gave the skinny guy a punch on the shoulder and he nearly pissed himself, his eyes big and round as he stuttered out what else he knew.

"Yeah, that's right. Lombardo got the diamonds from a fence out on the west coast. Paid him a third of what the rocks were worth and had the guy ship them out to this fellow who comes down from Chi. Paid him pretty good too. He is supposed to deliver the rocks when he comes to picks up the money.

"Then Lombardo is gonna call Farnworth and tell him he has the diamonds. There's a reward for them you know, five hundred thousand. But Lombardo is gonna say that isn't enough, he wants another five hundred thousand or he's gonna call the insurance company who paid off the claim and turn him in."

"So where do you fit in all this?" Pat turned toward Stills but before he could open his mouth I held up a finger and shushed him.

"He wants the reward. Five hundred thousand will fit nicely in his war chest which is about empty. He needs that money to work his campaign for the election." I finished and the red came back into Stills face.

"So what if I did. I've done nothing wrong. In fact, I planned on calling Detective Peterson when the time was right. We could knock out two birds with one stone."

"Before or after you got the stones." I said this in a low voice and Stills glared at me. "And how was you gonna do this?"

"I have ways." Stills' eyes narrowed, his fists clenched so tight his knuckles were white.

"Uh-huh."

Stills glared at me, his face and mouth tight.

"That's what I thought. The two hoods that tried to take me and Pat out on the parking lot, I suspect they were some of G's men. I say the two of them were doing the same thing we were, scoping Myer's place out. They tried to take me and Pat out but Pat winged him. He fell over the rail and took off up to the square where he killed a cabbie and took his cab. I just happened to come along and I bet he thought his luck had changed. He tried to take me out again and I beat him to the punch and guess what I found in his shirt pocket? A matchbook from the Horned Toad, a phone number in it. Guess who it belongs to?"

I showed him the matchbook and Stills' face went pale, his phone number written on the inside flap then said, "Or are you working with him?"

Stills' face went bright red and he stuttered, tried to get words out but his mouth wouldn't work right. He closed it and swallowed, a big lump made a trail down his throat and he licked his lips.

"This little shit was supposed to call me when he found out when the diamonds were coming in. Evidently, someone got to him." His voice was a rasp as he spoke, his eyes narrowed at Casper. Casper looked from me to him and then back at me, sweat rolled down his face and he licked his lips before he spoke.

"That guy, G, he caught me on the phone one night talking to Stills, told me he wanted to talk to me outside and waved a fin in front of me. I met him outside and he had a goon with him. The guy was as big as a mountain and he roughed me up a bit. G searched me and found the matchbook."

"Of all the stupid…" Stills started to say. I held up a

hand and Stills went silent.

"He asked who the number was for and I didn't say anything so the big guy shook me so hard my teeth rattled and said if I didn't answer I wouldn't be able to."

"So you told him." Stills said this in a low voice and Casper nodded.

"I wanna keep all my teeth," he said the sweat still trickling down his face, "so I told him and he made me a deal. I could keep my bones and teeth intact if I called him before I called you."

"So G knows when the man from Chi is coming."

"Just that he is coming Friday. When, I haven't found out yet." Casper looked at Stills and grinned.

Stills groaned. I laughed and shook my head. Stills had been busted and then sold out by his own informant, the payment being Casper could keep his bones and teeth whole. There was still the matter of Jenny and Jerry though so I asked Casper about them.

"This Jerry guy, he's a sharp nosed guy with slicked down hair?"

I nodded and Casper made a face.

"He's Lombardo's new driver, calls himself Lenny. Lombardo had him checked out and he passed inspection."

"New driver? Is he collecting the…"

Casper shook his head no and said, "He's just the driver. Lombardo's second in charge is the pickup man. Jerry is more of a bodyguard/driver than anything."

I nodded. The perfect setup. Jerry in the car driving from one pickup to the next and then onto Myer's for the drop off. Jerry had just let the pig out of the poke by shooting off his mouth.

Cary had just been in the wrong place at the wrong time. Had tried to help who he thought was a fellow drunk, a man he figured was going through the same hell he had. He didn't know the guy was just out on a hoot. Jerry's drunken pride had spilled what he was gonna do to Cary, boasted about it, even drew a map and explained the job to him. Then they had tried to buy him off, Cary refused. The next step was to make sure he stayed quiet. If I had of only gotten to Cary sooner.

"You did good Casper. Don't you think he did good Stills?" I looked over my shoulder at Stills and he grunted.

"What does Stills have on you Casper?" He looked at me and then at Stills, his eyes wide and showing fear. I stepped between him and Stills breaking Stills' eye contact with him. "What's he got on you?"

"Larceny. My damned brother-in-law said I stole a car. I didn't, the car was barrowed. My sister loaned it to me. My brother-in-law is a son of a bitch. Stills told me if I did this for him he would forget about it if I did what he asked me to." I nodded at Casper and turned toward Stills, his red face had come back.

"Well, I'd say he has paid his dues wouldn't you? I mean, forgive and forget right? Works both ways don't you think?"

"You bastard," Stills whispered at me.

"Yeah, I hear that a lot." I grinned at Stills and turned back to Casper. "You run along now Casper. Don't worry about your old friend the D.A. He won't bother you."

Casper stepped around me and kept his face toward Stills as he edged toward the door. Stills eyeballed him hard as he tossed the door open and scrambled out.

"Anything happens to him," I whispered stepping up behind Stills, "I'll go to the Feds and tell them everything that happened with a few of my own embellishments added."

"You sorry bastard," Stills growled at me.

"Don't repeat yourself Stills. Its bad grammar." I laughed and walked back over to Shelly's desk, sat down as Stills stood sulking and talking to Pat. The grin on Pat's face made me snicker.

***

The talk was about Pat keeping his mouth shut about what Stills had in mind. He really hadn't done anything illegal yet, the diamonds still in the hands of the delivery boy. After Stills left, Pat hooked a chair with his foot and pulled it over beside Shelly's desk, sat down in it and let out a long, slow breath.

"I doubt he'll bother either one of us again as long as he's in office." Pat grinned at me. I grinned back and nodded.

"He told me to nail that bastard G, arrest him if he resisted. I told him I'd try but if he tried to shoot his way out..."

"You know he will."

"Yeah, so does Stills. Something is not right still." Pat took out a deck of smokes and shook one loose. "Stills is working some other angle, something that will both gain him support money and favor with the people."

"You believe that?"

"Don't you?"

I smiled and Pat looked over the flame of his lighter as he lit his cigarette. He didn't say anything but he knew I knew something. That something I was keeping to myself.

***

I did some poking around to see if I could get a handle on G. Jenny was still working at the Toad, our little buddy Casper keeping an eye on her and reporting to me what was going on. I'd told Jimmy to inform him of what I wanted to make sure his larceny stayed gone. Plus, he was to get us the pickup times. Casper told me by Friday there would be close to a hundred thousand to transport which was more than there usually was. Lombardo had a good week.

I picked up a pencil and started to figure. Out of that

one hundred thousand, Lombardo would take his cut, maybe thirty thousand plus a little skim of ten. The other places would also take a cut, how much depending on what the take was for the week. I figured maybe seventy, eighty thousand would end up at the delivery point, and Myers taking his cut and the rest would be bagged up and turned over to the courier. The thing was I needed to know what time delivery would get to Myer's store, something Casper hadn't gotten yet.

I mean, I could set watch on the place but with what had happened the last time…I tossed the pencil on the pad and leaned back in my chair and rubbed my face, thinking about what Pat and I had discussed the last time he was here. Pat was partly right, something still wasn't right. Stills was about to lose it because of something, and I have a feeling it has nothing to do with replenishing his war chest for the election. I stood and started to leave. Shelly had already left for home and I was headed there also when I heard the front door open.

I walked to my office doorway and then stopped. The vision of loveliness that had entered was one I had seen before. Lombardo's secretary looked at me and smiled, the gal better looking than the last time I'd seen her. She had on a pencil skirt that fit her like a second skin and the sweater she wore did the same. Her rack strained against the material and threatened to bust through.

She had on a wide belt, one of those that cinched her waist tight and gave her an hourglass look. A yellow scarf was wrapped around her neck and her hair fell down to her shoulders in waves and curls. She smiled, red lips full and sensual, slightly parted to show a set of white, even teeth. She walked toward me and her body seemed to float, the movements soft and graceful and sexy as hell. I stepped back and let her enter my office, the back side of her looked even better.

I motioned to one of the chairs in front of my desk and

she gave me a sly smile and settled in the one beside my desk and crossed her legs, the sound of nylons rubbing together loud in the air. I walked around behind my desk and sat down, turned toward her and leaned on my desk, her hand opened her clutch purse and took out a silver cigarette case, liberated one and held it to her lips. I grinned and tossed a box of matches to her. She pouted her lips and took the matches and lit up.

"So to what do I owe this pleasure?" I leaned back, my hand close to my right side just in case.

"Well, remember, I said I would see you again?" She let the smoke roll out of her mouth as she talked. "Here I am."

"So you are and I ask again, why? Lombardo getting antsy?"

"Not hardly. No, I'm here for another party, one that wants me to tell you that if you don't keep your nose out of this, things could get nasty."

"Define nasty." I never let my eyes leave hers. She was good. My stare usually makes them sweat and this one wasn't.

"Let's just say certain parties are in my partner's sights and if those diamonds end up in any other hands but his, said parties will not fare too well." She took another puff, the smoke rolled out of her mouth as she smiled. I sat for a moment; my eyes still on hers and a wicked smile crossed my lips. I leaned forward, one hand on the desk top and the other close to my .45.

"You go tell this partner of yours," I said in a low voice, my eyes drilling her, "anything, *anything* happens to one certain party, I will find you both. You tell this other party that for me okay?"

My wicked smile got wider and my .45 was halfway out from under my coat. Now she was sweating, the cigarette between her fingers shook a little. She dropped her eyes then, stubbed out the cigarette and stood, smoothed her skirt and walked to the door, stopped and looked over her shoulder.

"You tell him," I hissed at her and pulled the .45 clear. She gave me a short nod and exited my office, the door closing as she left. Other party she had said. It could only be one of two left in this mess. Which I would find out in the long run and whichever one it was, they could find out just how nasty I could be.

CHAPTER 13

If there's one thing I don't like its threats, especially from a low life, but which low life. I spent the rest of the evening telling Shelly what was going on. Then I hit a couple of more people I knew to see if G had turned up anywhere. He was still in the wind. A couple of winos swore they saw him walking down the street around midnight, but as bombed as they were and with their bottle almost gone, they were just looking for more money. I got a cussing when I told them they were full of it and shoved the fin back in my pants.

Sleep evaded me as I tried to put all the pieces together, but there were still a few missing and probably wouldn't turn up until the heist went down. I'd have to be Jonny-on-the-spot when it did or everything would fall through and Cary would be just another unsolved murder. I wasn't going to let that happen. I went home, crawled into the bed and finally drifted off, Shelly waking me around noon and wanted to know if I was gonna sleep all day. I told her hell no and grabbed her, the girl didn't even struggle.

***

It was Wednesday night and with the warm weather the younger generation was coming out of their hibernation. Kids wandered around, some huddled in groups, others walking hand in hand spooning as the old-timers called it. A few cars were going up and down the street, hot rods to old beaters, the rumble of hopped-up engines echoing down the corridor of the street, kids yelling at each other as they passed. I shook my head and walked on. In a few minutes a couple of squad cars would show up, the kids would scatter and the street would get quiet again, the movie houses or the recreation halls catching the noise. Around midnight the drunks would start in and the noise would be back. Cars started and revved and gears ground as drunks headed out, wives picking up soused husbands and bitching them out for being drunk again. The husbands loud and obnoxious, telling them to shut the hell up and just drive.

This will go on all night until the bars close and then a few hours after. The rest of the drunks either stagger away home or try to drive home, the latter being the ones who ended up in the drunk tank at the Station, not a good place to be. Thursday and Friday it would start all over again but with more kids around.

I stepped into Kelso's and the crowd was light, the regulars already juiced up and the non-regulars headed that way. The pool table was covered, a sign hanging from the light above it saying the poolroom was closed. I laughed and walked over to Fisk's booth, the blonde I had seen him leave with the last time I was here sat beside him.

"Hey Max," Fisk said a smile on his face, "wondered when you would show back up."

"I've been busy," I answered him.

"So I heard. Max, this is Lilly, Lilly Max." Fisk waved a hand at her and then at me. It was the first time I ever saw him grin so much.

"Hello Max." Her voice was velvet soft when she spoke, her eyes fluttered and she held out a hand. I shook it lightly and then slid in across from the two of them.

"Say babe," Fisk handed her a bunch of quarters, "go check out the jukebox and see if there is anything worth playing on it."

"I take its boys time?" She had a pout on her face and Fisk nodded.

"I'll make it up to you later." Fisk patted her arm and she slid out of the seat, the dress she wore tight and accented her figure perfectly. She did a little wiggle as she smoothed it down and bent down toward him, her cleavage deep and her dress straining to keep her Balcony in.

"Okay sweet cheeks." She straightened and walked toward the jukebox, her hips swaying and every male eye glued to them.

"Sweet cheeks huh?" Fisk cut his eyes toward me and shook his head.

"Yeah, and if you know what's good for you, you'll keep it to yourself."

"Cross my heart," I said making a motion across my chest and he grunted.

"I can see hell freezing over first. What's on your mind?"

"I had a visitor a little while ago, a dark haired beauty that sits at the desk outside Lombardo's office." I leaned on the table and Fisk nodded.

"Uh-huh, her name is Linda and she isn't Lombardo's receptionist, she's his sister," Fisk said.

"That explains the threat then?"

"Oh?"

"Yeah, she told me to back off or people could get hurt. She told me it was other parties but if she is Lombardo's spawn then…"

"I got news for you buddy, she didn't mean

Lombardo."

"Come again?"

"Linda and Lombardo had a falling out the last time you seen her, one that involves three stones and a guy in a tweed suit."

"G."

"The one and only. He met her at The Toad. Rumor is she was a little loose, talked a lot and told G about her stupid brother grabbing some diamonds an old friend had lost and offered a reward for. Seems the insurance has already paid out on the claim and now her brother has his old friend by the balls. Later G came to her and struck a deal."

"What kind of deal?"

"She also told him where they were to be delivered and that Lombardo is going to give a donation to someone in the D.A.s office to keep the law away from them or certain pictures would be handed over to the papers if he didn't."

"Blackmail. No wonder Stills was so hard on my and Pat's ass."

"Uh-huh."

"Any word on which route the pickup man will be taking?"

"Been doing some poking around yourself huh?" Fisk said. A grin crossed his face.

"Can't let you have all the fun."

"Uh-huh. That one has been a little harder. The person you talked to probably told you of two routes, there is a third one. My guess is it will be the one that is taken this time. The man along with a partner is coming down from Chi, the partner picked up along the way. The two hoods pick them up. He and his buddy gets a little bonus for their trouble."

"And if the boys from Chi find out?" I grinned and Fisk chuckled.

"I know that tone." I stood and held out my hand, Fisk

waving it off. "This one is a freebie, just let me know how it turns out unless I hear it first."

***

I made a call to Chicago to a fellow I knew who was connected to the Big Boys there. I explained to him what was going down. There was a long pause on the other end and then he laughed.

"I have heard hints that something was going down but those that have instigated it have been keeping it close," he sighed.

"I thought you guys knew everything that went on in your part of the world?"

There was a grunt and then he said, "Most things Max, important things like when there is about to be an upset. This isn't something that rates that high."

"Diamonds worth millions of dollars don't rate?"

"My dear Max, that is small time compared to the other transactions that take place. The thing that upsets us is the way it is done."

"Meaning behind your backs?"

"Exactly."

"So would you like me to take care of this little infraction for your people?"

There was a long pause on the other end, the only thing heard being his breathing and a muted tap, which was probably his fingernail on the big desk he sat behind.

"Yes, that will suffice."

"I'll need the route he's going to take."

"There are two he usually takes but I'd say for this one he will take another that is more out of the way, especially if he is to pick up the diamonds along the way. Let me check and see if it is the one. I'll call you back when I find out."

We talked for a bit more, then he hung up.

Shelly came in after I finished and sat down in the chair by my desk, a questioning look on her face.

"What's up kitten?" I leaned back and waited for her to talk.

"The man on the phone, was that…"

I nodded and she had a shocked look on her face. I smiled and leaned forward on my desk.

"Gary, as he likes to be known as these days, owes me a favor. I kept a bullet from ending his career early one time. This will square it between us." I said. "Gino Pirelli was a young hood back when I was on the police force up in St. Louis. We were both young and stupid then, Gino muscling in on the rackets another fellow was running. There had been a showdown the night we met, ten or twenty guys shot it out in a warehouse over on the east side. To tell the truth, I had mistaken him for one of the warehouse workers and when a hood from the other side lay a bead on him I downed the guy, Gino taking off. It was later, when he saw me in a drugstore that he came over and thanked me. Told me if I ever needed a favor to just call."

"But he's…one of the bad guys."

I shrugged and Shelly shook her head. What she didn't know was I had a lot of connections that were less that honorable, some owed me favors and some just respected me and the way I did things to steer clear. Most of these connections were made in my early days, St. Louis streets the place where one can meet the most interesting people. An hour later the phone rang. Shelly answered it and after five minutes came into my office and handed me a piece of paper.

"Gino?" I asked.

She nodded and said, "He told me that and then he asked when we were going to get married? I told him soon and he said to tell you to send him an invitation. He also said that you two were even."

I chuckled and she sat down in the chair beside my

desk again, a look of worry on her face. I dropped the paper on my desk and leaned toward her, cupped her chin in my hand and squeeze it.

"Not to worry sweet cheeks. Gino is old school and though the debt is repaid, he still respects me. He just wants to send us a little wedding present."

"What, a bomb?"

I laughed and shook my head. "Whatever it is it won't explode." She stood shook her head and went back out into her office. Most people believed the Big Boys to be all evil, gun toting mad men who do evil things. Some of them were but a lot of them weren't. A lot of them were keeping the younger generation that was coming up in the ranks from polluting the organization with bad ideas. One of those ideas was the sale of drugs. The old Dons forbid it but that doesn't mean it wasn't happening.

I looked down at the paper Shelly had handed me and it told me that the courier would leave Thursday afternoon, which would put him in the city around midnight or after, spend the day there and then around midnight Friday night, pick up the money. Gino had given me his route also. It also said word had come down that he was making an unauthorized stop along the way, probably for the rocks. Evidently someone was keeping tabs on what Lombardo was doing. I grunted and picked up the phone then hung it back up. A plan shot into my mind, one that would involve Shelly and a flat tire.

**

Thursday Night.

Planter's Road was more or less the scenic route into Springfield during the daytime. At night it was a dark and shadowed one lane road. It bypassed the main road and wound around through the countryside till it eventually wound back up on the main highway. A gravel road that was filled with pot holes and ripples, a couple of low water bridges and lots of sharp rocks to put holes in worn out tires. Shelly and I left out just before dark, my old beater shook and bounced as we drove along the road and came to the first low water bridge. I turned the car around and parked it on the shoulder, crawled out and let the air halfway out of the driver's side back tire.

I jacked the car up and then told Shelly now there was the wait and handed her my flashlight.

"What if he's already come through?" Shelly's voice was soft, her eyes big as she looked around. Night in the city is nothing like night in the country. In the city there is always some kind of noise. Cars rolling down the streets and houses lit up. Here it is quiet, the only sounds in the air being crickets and other animals that were wandering about. I grinned and told her not to worry, I'd be close in case the booger man tried to get her. She called me a name and swung the flashlight at me. I jumped back and laughed.

That thought had also occurred to me as we drove out there but if my calculations were right, the Chi man wouldn't be along until just after dark, the roads more deserted than in the daytime. Being farm country, farmers traveled the roads and a fancy car would draw attention. I took a cigar from my vest and lit up, watching the road north for a set of headlights. I took a drag and then Shelly took it from me, the butt shaking as she took a puff. I grinned and waved it off when she tried to give it back, took out another and lit up.

"You know, there used to be a house up on that ridge," I said pointing at where the dimming sky and the ridge met, the face of it black as midnight. "A couple of brothers lived up there, albinos, white as ghosts when they were seen at night. Seems they got in a fight one night over a woman they both wanted to marry. They found their bodies here at the bridge, hands locked around each other's throats and their faces twisted up in hate. Ever since then, if a woman comes to the bridge or her car breaks down and she is alone, those two brothers are seen by her, hands locked around each other's throats, faces twisted and eyes hollow, rising up out of the water and coming toward her moaning their beloved's name."

Right then an owl hooted and Shelly jumped, the cigar in her fingers hit the road and she damned near flew into my arms. I couldn't help it, I laughed and she gave me a cussing and was still mumbling a few choice words when I saw the headlights. I hoped it wasn't some farmer out on a hoot but the car sounded too smooth to be a farm heap. I motioned to Shelly and then slipped behind the car, dropped my cigar and ground it out and pulled my .45 out as the headlights got closer.

Lady luck was on our side as a dark colored Buick pulled to a stop a foot from my old heap. I ducked down to stay out of the headlights as one of the car doors, the driver's side, opened up and a figure stepped out, the smell of expensive cologne touched my nose. Shelly pulled her coat tight around her, playing the part of a helpless woman stranded on a country back road.

"Problem?" I couldn't see the guy's face as he walked toward her, his back was to the headlights and his front was in shadow.

"Thank God, I'm so glad you came along," Shelly panted as she spoke. "I've a flat tire and I can't get the lug nuts loose to change it."

The man stepped forward and Shelly stepped back, her coat held tight but one hand under it wrapped around the butt of her .357.

"Not to worry." He picked up the lug wrench and started to loosen the nuts, the other car door opening and a fellow crawled out of the passenger side and walked toward them.

"What the hell are you doing Lonny?" The second guy growled at the first, the first guy looked up and growled back. There were two of them when there was only supposed to be one, why I couldn't guess and didn't. I just hoped Shelly didn't freeze when things popped. She was still a little shook over her last encounter at the office.

"The lady needs a hand dumbass."

"We got a schedule to keep buddy," the second one hissed back.

"We'll be on time, don't worry about it." The first guy grunted and went back to working on the tire. I had eased around in the dark and came to the back of the Buick and crouched as he walked back to the car door. He struck a match, the flair of the flame lighting up his cigarette fading as he turned his back to me and started to open the door. I was behind him in two steps. He must have heard the gravel crunch under my feet, hard to be quiet on a gravel road, and spun, the muzzle of my .45 thumped him on the head and I caught him before he hit the ground. I let him down slow and then walked up to the front of their car. The guy working on the tire grunted and cussed under his breath. I stepped past the headlights and he growled at me and turned his head thinking it was his buddy.

"I said…" he didn't finish the sentence, Shelly's .357's muzzle planted itself in the back of his head and he froze. Guess she was over the incident.

"Stand up easy buddy, I can't guarantee what will happen if you move too fast." I grinned and he stood slowly, his hands out and away from his body. I frisked him down and took a 9mm out from under his arm and shoved it in my belt then stepped in close, the muzzle of my .45 touching him under the chin.

"The stones, where are they?" He swallowed and pointed at the car.

"In the front seat, small brown paper package."

"He moves, kill him." I stepped back, the muzzle of Shelly's piece nudged him a little and even though I couldn't see his face I could tell he was sweating. I walked back to the car and opened the passenger door, the interior lights showing me the package on the front seat. I took it out and lay my .45 on the roof of the car then opened the package. It was about the size of a watch box. I opened it and let out a low whistle. Three diamonds were nestled inside, three flawless rocks that reflected what light there was in the night. I closed the box and slipped it in my pocket, picked up my .45 and started to walk back to Shelly.

I guess it wasn't my time yet because there was a shot and both door glasses shattered as a slug burned a path across the back of my coat. I spun and fired, the hood I had knocked out had come to. He never got off a second shot, my .45 barked and the back of his head splattered the night air with bones and blood. I heard Shelly yelp and turned, hood number one had his arm around her throat, her pistola jammed in her side.

"Pretty smart but not smart enough." He poked Shelly hard in the ribs and grinned. "Drop the rod."

I dropped my .45 on the road and he grinned wider. "Now the stones, give 'em here."

I reached into my pocket and he gave her another poke so I reached in slow and pulled them out and tossed them on the road in front of them. He snorted and shook his head.

"No, pick 'em up and bring 'em to me."

I shrugged and started to take a step, Shelly raised her foot and slammed it down hard on the hood's instep then jerked away from him. I stooped, scooped up my .45 and pulled the trigger, three slugs hit him in the chest, knocking him backward till he tripped and fell. I walked over and knelt down beside him, his eyes glazed and his hand loose around her .357. I pulled it from his hand and walked back to Shelly and handed it to her.

"Good thing I wore spikes huh?" She looked up at me and her face was pale. I took her in my arms and hugged her tight till she stopped shaking then changed the tire and tossed the bodies in their car, drove it off in the ditch and then we headed for home.

CHAPTER 14

The newspapers and radio went nuts the next morning. Two bodies were found on Planter's Road by a farmer, both looked as if they had been shot, one in the head and the other in the chest. The county sheriff said both men were criminals and it was probably an execution. Far from it. I folded the paper and tossed it on my desk, the stones setting in front of me in the center. I'm sure G had probably figured out what had happened on the road and was mad as hell. He no doubt thought it was Jerry and Jenny. More the better he thought that. It would bring him to Myer's store when they heisted the money to get the diamonds and I would have all three of them.

I tapped the top of the box and mulled over an idea in my mind, then picked up the phone and called a friend of mine. The phone rang six times before it was answered, the man on the other end a little out of breath.

"Milford's Jewelry," the voice spoke on the other end catching his breath.

"Hello Stan, just get in or training the new help?" I grinned as the man on the other end muttered a curse then cleared his throat and spoke.

"If I knew it was you I'd of let it ring," Milford growled.

"Now, now Stan, lets not start the day off with a frown."

There was a pause on the other end and I could hear a foot kick the door closed.

"What the hell do you want Max?" I grinned on my end and did a pause of my own. Stan's wife told him that every morning before he left for work. Stan was not a morning man but he never said anything to her. She would cuff him upside the head if he did. She'd do more than cuff him upside the head if she knew how he was training his new employees, the female ones anyway.

"I was wondering if you had any of those fake rocks still around?"

Another pause then Stan said, "I may have, why?"

"I need some of them."

"For what?"

"I'll tell you when I see you." I hung up the phone and laughed. Stan had gotten in some fake diamonds about a year ago, cheaper for those who didn't have the money for the real thing. They were as good as the real thing, some even more so. One of his saleswomen knew this and had been selling them as the real deal and Stan caught her but not before she had flown the coop with the money. Stan had been accused as an accomplice and his wife had hired me to find the girl. I found her and Stan ducked the bullet, his salesgirl got a year in the women's pen upstate. I grabbed up the box and my trench coat and headed out the door, Stan my next stop.

Stan's shop was right by the Fox Theater, a small hole in the wall store that did a good business. When I walked in he was waiting on a customer and his new girl asked if she could help me. That was a loaded question. She was medium height, curvy and well endowed. She had a cute face with full red lips which I suspect drove the boys crazy to kiss them. I leaned on the counter and smiled.

"You must be Stan's new help?" My smile widened and she smiled back. "How long you been here?"

"About two weeks," she answered.

"You like working for him?"

"Yeah, except in the morning. He's an old grump."

I chuckled and glanced over my shoulder at Stan, he was trying to keep one eye on me and one on the customer.

"Want me to tell you how to solve that problem?" She nodded and I looked at him again. He was trying to hurry the customer up and not having too good a luck at it. I gave him a smile over my shoulder and he looked daggers at me. I turned back to the girl, opened my mouth to speak and Stan was beside me.

"Kelly, go help Miss Murdock check out." I looked over at him, the dagger look still in his eyes, a snicker coming from my lips.

"Nice to meet you, Mr.,..."

"Black, nice to meet you too." She hustled off toward the woman and I leaned out to watch her walk toward the customer. I let out a low whistle and raised my eyebrows at Stan and shook my head.

"Hope you didn't tell her anything that would get her fired," he growled at me.

"Nope, you got here too quick." I stood up straight and Stan shook his head.

"Let's talk in the back." Stan motioned for me to follow and as I stepped past the girl by the register, I winked at her and she giggled. Stan has a repair shop in the back, he fixes loose settings and does some watch work. I leaned on a counter where he was working on a piece of jewelry, some of the stones out of the settings. He slid up on a stool and I leaned against the table he worked on, his eyes watching me.

Stan is a tall, lanky man with big hands and thick

fingers. How he fixes watches with those sausage fingers is beyond me. His clothes fit him loose, a pair of suspenders holds his pants up and his shoes are scuffed. He has a long face with a long nose, a knob on the end of it and almost no chin. His hair is thinning. His attempt at hiding it being to let it grow long on one side and comb it over the bald spot. I bet he has a tough time when it's a windy day.

"So why are you here?" His voice was low and his lips barely moved when he spoke. I reached in my pocket and pulled out the box, handed it to him and nodded at it. Stan gave me a funny look then flipped the box open, his face went slack and he let out a low whistle.

"Are these…"

"Yeah." He turned toward the table and lay the box down gently, fitted an eyepiece in his eye and picked up one of the diamonds. He turned it slowly and carefully, the light above the table catching the facets and reflecting the light. After a few minutes, looking at all three diamonds, he let the eyepiece fall out into his hand and looked at me.

"How the hell did you get these, no, I don't want to know." He shook his head, "You know there is a reward out for the return of these."

"Yeah, I know. I thought only the dregs of society knew about that?"

"They do, but guys like me hear stuff."

"Uh-huh."

"So why bring them to me?"

"I need some fakes, something that's as close as you can get to the looks of these. I want to catch some rats with them." He gave me another funny look and slid off the stool.

"I got some synthetic crap back here I use when people want to take the real stuff out in case the jewelry gets stolen. Let's take a look and see what I got."

He went back to a cabinet, pulled out a tray that, to the common eye, looked like it held the real thing. He set the tray down and poked through the boxed off sections, picked out three that were almost exactly like the ones in the box and set them side by side with the ones in the box. They were close, damned close. Only an expert could tell the difference and he would have to look real close.

"How much?" I reached for my wallet and Stan waved me off.

"The things are worth no more than a dollar a piece. Just tell me what you plan to really do with them."

I did and as I did a smile grew on his face. He picked up the fakes and put them in a small, black pouch then handed me them and the box. I thanked him and exited the store, passed by the little gal and she gave me a sexy smile. Man, if I wasn't connected and ten years younger…

***

I got back to the office after dark. Shelly was still there doing some filing when I walked in. She was leaning over the top drawer, her skirt tight against her back side and her hair covering part of her face. She looked over at me as I walked in, a slight smile on her face and a wicked gleam in her eyes. The girl is a knock out and I am lucky to have her. She could have had any other Joe in this town. Most of the guys I know had asked her out a few times.

Now they are jealous. Now they wondered why she wanted an old, broken-down number like me. I usually tell them I'm an exciting guy and they just snort. She is a dream, long legs curving up into shapely hips, descending into a perfect waist then exploding into a balcony that makes heads turn. Her face is heart shaped with a cute chin and a pixie nose. Her lips are full and red, the kind a guy wants to kiss and kiss so hard they hurt. Yeah, my kitten, think I'll keep her.

She closed the cabinet drawer and walked over to me, her skirt swishing against those lovely legs and tossed her arms around me, kissed me and then leaned back, her eyes telling me she missed me. I gave her a hug and then pulled loose, my hand holding the black pouch which I showed her. We went back in my office and I sat down, took the box out and opened it. The rocks inside catching the light and flashing back radiance. Shelly picked the box up and stared at them for a moment. She had seen them before but not up close.

What is it about diamonds that makes a woman stare and flush as they look at them? I've mulled this over a couple of times in my head and even asked a couple of ladies what the fascination was. Most of them told me it was their radiance, the luster of a stone cut to perfection, reflecting the light, flashing it back at them and making them wonder what it would be like to own them. Shelly reached up and let her hand hover over the stones for a second, reached down and touched them lightly, caressed them, her eyes bright with fascination. I opened the pouch and dumped the fakes on the top of my desk. Her eyes glanced down at them then back to the real ones.

"Five million dollars," she said almost in a whisper, "three stones made from lumps of coal. How in hell can they be worth so much?"

She picked up one of the fakes, looked it over and set it back down, her eyes going from the real to the fake.

"What do you think? Think they will fool G?" I watched her and she tapped her chin, her eyes darted back and forth as she scanned the rocks.

"Well, if he doesn't look real good I think they will." She looked at me and I grinned.

"I was hoping you'd say that." I picked the real ones up one at a time and dropped them in the empty pouch, pulled the string in the top and closed it. "Now, I need you to hide these until this is all over, somewhere G won't think to look."

Shelly took the pouch and held it in her hand for a

second, a slow smile crossing her face as she nodded. I knew she had a spot, probably one that I would have trouble finding. I picked up the fakes and placed them in the box, closed the lid, leaned back and checked my watch. Tonight I would put my plan into effect. One last detail needed to be done so I picked up the phone and dialed Pat, the switchboard operator at the station connected me and we talked for a while. Mostly he listened and when I was done he told me he would be ready. I hung up and leaned back in my chair. This should be a walk in the park unless something happened. I just hoped Lady Luck was still on my side.

***

From my office I watched the street. Most of the people had either gone home or were busy drinking away their paychecks. For a Friday night it was pretty dead but there was a dance down at the VA Hall so I figured things were hopping down that way. Better no one was around in case something went wrong. Around eleven a big, dark colored Ford came down the street, slid to the curb and a well-dressed fellow got out, went into the building two doors down from my office, the tailor shop, and then came out ten minutes later, a duffle bag in his hand. I grinned and waited until the car started up and took off before I moved.

I made tracks to the parking lot across from my office, fired up my old heap and eased it out onto the street, the Ford turning the corner as I headed toward him. I took it slow and easy until I got to the corner then turned, a couple of squad cars, no lights or sirens nosed into the curb in front of the tailor shop and did their thing.

The second stop was at a pawn shop so I made a turn into a service alley one door down and cut my motor, the car pulled to a stop beside a car parked at the curb and the guy got out, spent fifteen minutes inside and then came out with another duffle bag, this one a little bigger than the first. He crawled in as the driver shoved the car in gear and headed toward the alley. I started mine and eased on down, as the hood nosed into the alley. I drove on and hoped he figured I was some drunk looking for a place to sleep it off so I pulled on down, let my car jerk to a stop and watched him in my mirror.

He slowed down and turned onto a one lane road hidden by some bushes that ran behind the buildings along Booneville Street, shifted his heap down into granny and eased down. I crawled out and walked back to the road. I hadn't seen it when I passed it, the road no more than a graveled cow path. I drew my .45 and checked to see if one was in the chamber then started down the road. Bushes and a couple of trees gave me good cover as I made my way toward Myer's store.

I was halfway there when I heard another car, this one's engine made no more noise than a whisper as the car slowed and turned onto the road. I slid behind some bushes and waited, the car passing, the one at the wheel a blonde. I grinned and let her get past me and slipped out into the shadows. The car pulled to a stop and a fellow smoking a cigarette walked over to her. They talked for a few minutes then she crawled out of the car, handed him a trench gun and the two of them headed to the back door.

I was about to move again and another car pulled in, lights off, this one as quiet as the first. I slipped back into the shadows and watched as the car slowed to a stop.

Once they were inside, the door opened and fellow got out. This one had to be G. I watched as he reached back in the car and pulled out a trench gun himself, jacked a shell in the chamber and walked down to the store. I waited, the pause long, voices suddenly heard from inside the store. Trench guns boomed and men screamed, one of them staggered out the back door, his shirt front dark and his hands clawed at his face. I started to run toward the ruckus, the first one that stepped out of the doorway would go down and I hoped it was G. I was almost to the door when something else happened. I heard glass shatter, voices yelled to lay down their weapons and then gunfire.

G came flying out the back door, fired off a blast and then turned. He was quick I'll have to give him that. The minute he saw me he fired off another round, the pellets hissing past me as I opened up. G stumbled then righted himself, fired off another blast and took off the other way. I fired twice more. He stumbled again then made the corner of the building where the railroad tracks ran.

He was halfway down them when I came out and started to take him down. It didn't happen. The chatter of a pepper box sizzled the air with slugs. I hit the cinders and rolled up next to the building, an old barrel catching hell as I lay there. Then it was gone, the sound of a car revving and the squall of tires biting pavement loud in the night air. I jumped up and ran, made it to the street in time to see taillights headed north toward Commercial Street

CHAPTER 15

Stills was inside giving orders to Pat as I walked back to Myer's backdoor. He was red in the face, breathing heavy and growling at the men who were securing the scene. I stepped back outside, lit a cigar and puffed on it as Pat walked up to me. We walked over to the first car and leaned on it, his hands went in his coat pockets and a frown crossed his face.

"How bad?" My voice was low, almost a growl.

"All five bought it, Jenny and Jerry, Myers, Lombardo's delivery boy and the pickup man. All five got a load of buckshot up close and personal."

"And the money?"

"Most of it still in the duffel bags, what was on the table was scattered when Myers fell across it."

"So how did Stills find out about this?"

Pat shrugged and said, "Probably somebody in the department. He sent word down that *he* was gonna handle this one. I guess he thought he could still get the stones. What about G?"

"He took one or two from me then beat it to the

railroad tracks. I guess he planned ahead because there was a car in the front waiting for him. They took off north."

"He have the diamonds?"

I grinned and shook my head as I said, "Probably, but not the ones he wanted."

"What's that supposed to mean?"

"The pickup man dropped by to see me earlier this afternoon. One of Gino's boys. I gave him a package. Too bad too, the rocks in the package were fakes."

"You old bastard, where are the real ones?"

"Safe." I said this in a low voice and nodded toward the backdoor, Stills stood there talking to a uniform. Pat bounced off the car and chuckled.

"Hell, I wish he could've at least left one alive to see who killed Cary." He walked toward the door, his hands still in his pockets as Stills met him. Still's eyes glared at me as I bounced off the car and gave him a wave.

***

It was supposed to be the perfect set up. G, Jenny and Jerry and Lombardo's boy all in one place. Gino's man was supposed to help me collar them but G had seen Stills busting in the front door and ruined the whole thing. G had killed him and the others before I could get there. I hoped Gino would understand. I crawled back in my car and started it up, pulled out onto the street and headed back to my office. I'm sure G would figure out pretty fast who had the stones once he got a good look at them and he would be coming after me. That is, if he wasn't suffering from a .45 slug in him.

I pulled into the lot across from my office, slid out of my car and headed toward the street when the muzzle of a pistol touched the back of my neck, the voice that spoke raspy and pained.

"One move and I'll kill you!" It was G, the coppery

smell of blood touched my nose as he nudged me forward. "Careful, I may be hurt but I can still blow your head off in the blink of an eye."

"Where we headed?" I asked.

"To your office. Move!" I did what he said. The two of us crossed the street and he groaned a little but the pressure on the back of my neck remained. On the sidewalk I started to take out my keys and noticed the door was partway open so I gave it a push and a voice, velvet smooth called out.

"Back here, any false moves and your whore gets it in the head."

Linda. Dark haired and sexy Linda. Not so sexy now, her face twisted up in rage. In her hand was a .357 aimed at Shelly's head. Shelly's eyes were big and she started to speak but I waved her off. The less she said the better. G kept his pistola snug against the back of my neck, his breath coming in ragged gasps. The smell of blood stronger.

"The diamonds," Linda said in a hard voice, "where are they?"

I gave her a nasty smile and shrugged. "I thought G had them." She cocked the hammer of the .357.

"Those were fakes you son of a bitch." G's breath was labored as he spoke, his words came out forced. "I checked them in the car and they were fakes. You have them, so where are they?"

He cocked his pistola and I felt his hand shake. Linda stopped him from pulling the trigger, her voice still smooth as silk as she spoke.

"Easy G, let's not do something stupid till we find out where they are." Her eyes were locked on him and he hesitated for a few seconds then eased off. "Like he said, where are they?"

"Safe." I gave her a nasty smile and she gave Shelly's head a hard nudge.

"Wrong answer. One last chance then I blow her brains

out. Where are they?"

My smile got wider and Shelly's eyes did too. She knew I was gonna do a stall and hope I could make Linda mad enough to make a mistake.

"Does big brother know what you're doing?" I asked suddenly, Linda's face twisted more, "because I figure he has already got a call from the boys in Chi wanting to know what the hell he is doing."

"So let them call. He already had an excuse made up to give them." Linda's voice was a low hiss.

"Really? And did that excuse include the money that was to be heisted along with the diamonds, money and diamonds both disappearing before you could come out looking like the good guy, take out the bad guy and as a reward gain control of the casino?" It was a long shot but it paid off. Linda stared at me and her hand shook. Shelly was sweating a little, drops of it cutting tracks in her makeup.

"What the hell is that supposed to mean?"

"G here," I said shifting my eyes back at G without moving my head and then back to her, "he *is* a master planner remember? Everything that has happened has been instigated by the man himself. Hell, and I bet you thought it was all your idea."

It was a bluff, most of the pieces I had but some were still a little fuzzy so I put on my detective face and talked.

"G was the one who was supposed to heist the diamonds from Farnsworth in the first place but got stepped on when Jenny and her hubby Jerry ran a scam on the old man and when that fell through, Jerry cracked the safe and grabbed the jewelry. They got it fenced but the kid who fenced it took off with their money leaving them high and dry.

"In the meantime, the old man collects the insurance but wants the rocks back, probably sentimental value and offers a reward on the sly for the recovery of them. Five hundred g's to *anyone* who can get them back. G's on the hunt now and finds out Lombardo has acquired them, but doesn't have them. G finds this out from the kid who fenced the stuff for them. G tracked him down through his contacts and caught him at the bus station ready to make tracks to California with the money. He finds out who has the stones from the kid and slits his throat, takes the money but by the time he gets to the fence, Lombardo's contacts already have the rocks and the fence ends up like the kid, dead.

"The two J's read about the kid in the papers and figure they are shit out of luck until Jenny gets wind that the rocks were bought by Lombardo so her and Jerry make tracks back here, the guy who gave her the information between the sheets telling her about Lombardo's casino and how much money it made. Together they planned the heist and came back here to case out the casino and find out when would be the best time to hit the green and the rocks."

I paused for a moment, Linda stared past me at G and G at her. I figured I had hit the nail on the head so I continued.

"So Jenny gets a job at The Horned Toad and Jerry pulls in a few favors to get on Lombardo's team, Jenny watching the casino until Jerry's credentials clear the hood background check. That's how Jenny met G, at The Toad. She knew who he was and contacted him about maybe helping them with their plan a little better. He agreed. In the meantime, Jerry is whooping it up and gets drunk, brags about what he is gonna do to my friend Cary. Even draws him a map and tells him how it is gonna go down.

"In the meantime, G notices Lombardo talking with you one night, must have been an argument because it got rough and G, thinking maybe you are one of Lombardo's honeys and gets real chummy with you. Probably buys you drinks and while he is trying to get some information out of you finds out you're Lombardo's sister which makes his plan just that much better."

"His plan?" Linda cut in. I nodded and G leaned up behind me and hissed a warning in my ear. I smiled and plowed on.

"Uh-huh. Wasn't it him who told you to go off Cary?"

"I offered him a piece of the action. I didn't want to kill the kid but he told me it wasn't right so I had to." She hissed this at G more than me, her eyes shot daggers at him.

"Uh-huh," I nodded, "all this was to get the diamonds, but to also snag the money. See, Lombardo has been laundering G's money for him, didn't know that did you? Like the armored car hold up down in Dallas, How much that net you G?"

"None of your business," he answered me. "The diamonds, where are they?"

His pistol pushed hard into the back of my head and his breath was hot and filled with the stink of blood. Shelly looked at me and in her eyes I could see fear. Maybe I had pushed too far with G and was about to make a move, good or bad, when Linda hissed at him.

"Answer him G." Her voice was a whisper and her eyes were deadly. G looked at her and laughed.

"Two hundred thousand dollars. Your brother screwed me over my dear. Out of all that money I got only forty thousand. His excuse was he would have to funnel it through various banks a little at a time. Most of the money would be spent in payoffs to those involved. I knew that was a lie but one doesn't go up against the *Big Boys* as this shamus puts it. I have waited for a time when I could recoup at least half of what he stole from me back. Tonight would have been the night but this piece of shit ruined it!"

G groaned and the gun lightened up a bit on my neck. I moved but G wasn't that far gone. He punched the muzzle of his rod back against my neck hard and I flinched.

"And the diamonds?" Linda asked.

"My dear, they were to be the coup de grace of the

plan. With those and the money I could disappear and live life to the fullest." He said this with a nasty tone. Linda's eyes narrowed more.

"In other words you sorry bastard," Linda hissed, "you planned on taking it all."

"Since you put it that way…yes."

Linda screamed and when she did I ducked and gave G an elbow. He folded and as he did I grabbed Shelly and dove toward my desk. G cussed as Linda pulled the trigger, he had enough strength left to duck and Linda's bullet clipped the top of his shoulder. He fired just as she was ready to pull off another shot. His slug caught her in the throat, her eyes going wide as she reached up and touched her neck. Her hand came back red, her eyes rolled up and she fell to the floor.

"Remember what I said about you being a dumb son of a bitch," I said as he turned toward me. "You forgot this."

He started to speak and then he saw the .45 in my hand. He had forgotten to relieve me of it. His eyes went wide for a moment and then he let out a high whine, the sound cut off as my pistola coughed lead, the back of his head decorating the wall behind him. One of these days I need to get some of that new wall paint, the kind that just wipes clean. It's costing me a fortune to have this office repainted.

CHAPTER 16

I received a call a couple of days after this mess was over. It was Gino who told me not to worry about his man, things happen. As for Lombardo, he had been talked to and told his next delivery had better be all of the money or heads would roll, literally. Stills was laying low, the pictures he had worried so much about being nothing more than a few shots of him in the casino with a redhead on his arm and guess who that red head was. No doubt he had participated in some shenanigans other than strutting around with her but the proof wasn't there so he went back to his bossy ways until I told him I had copies of the 'other' pictures with the red head. I bet his wife would be happy to see those. It was a bluff naturally but he didn't know that.

Shelly was out of the office for a few days, a vacation so to speak. She had stared old man death in the face and came out of it. Hell, it scares everybody at one time or the other, sometimes it takes a little longer. The diamonds were turned over to the Feds and the Feds went to see Farnworth but the old man wasn't available and wouldn't be. He had died of heart failure a week before everything came to a head. His son had sold the business and fled the country, the five million and the money for the sale of the company in his pocket. Not a surprise since the family was almost broke.

The real surprise came when a check came to Father Mason, one totaling over one hundred thousand dollars. The name on the bottom line was Gary Pirelli, a donation in the name of Cary. To help the unfortunate to clean their lives up and make good in the world. Mason asked me about the name and I smiled, told him to deposit the check and forget about it. He did and the old building that was once an eyesore was now getting a makeover.

Jack had returned at the end of the week, the kid looking fit and ready for the world. Evidently Shelly had been talking to him and one warm night we sat out on the front porch, cigars stoked and the sounds of the city muffled but heard.

"Shelly tell you I was thinking about hanging it up?" I blew smoke and watched him, his head nodded and he looked at me.

"She said you wanted to take on a partner until he learned the ropes then turn the business over to him?"

"You interested?"

"Depends?"

"Depends on what?"

He turned toward me and had a big grin on his face.

"That you let me question the lookers."

"She put you up to that right?"

"Yeah, and I covered your ass, told her we would share the responsibility."

"How did that set with her?" I looked at him and returned the grin. He chuckled and looked over his shoulder then back at me.

"The word traitor came up in the conversation."

We both laughed.

ABOUT THE AUTHOR

Author Ike Keen

Ike Keen likes the tough guys. So tough guys are what he writes about.

He has been writing since 1986 and started off in the horror field. He's had short stories published in Fright Depot, Sterling Web and Black Pedals. However, soon he decided to go a different route by trying his hand in hardboiled detective stories. Mickey Spillane and Max Allen Collins are a couple of his favorite authors. He's adapted to that old school style, and made it his own.

Retired from the Springfield Public Schools, he now lives in a rural Missouri town. He hopes to include the setting in one of his future novels.

Keep an eye out for the next two novel's in the Max Black series.

AUTHOR'S NOTE

This is the third, but not last of the Max Black novels. I have enjoyed writing about him and his exploits, his sexy girlfriend and all the trouble he can get himself into. He is my first and I will always be true to him. I have penned a short tale about another detective, this one not as well liked as Max but just as tough, living in a tough part of the city.

The story takes place in the present and the main character I have had on the back burner for some time now. The story some might think is old hat but it gives you an idea of what the next tough guy is going to be like. I present him to you for your reading pleasure. Let me know what you think. He is another one of my favorites, then again, all my tough guys are.

HELL TOWN, USA

Hell Town.

The lower east side of the city. The place where all the crud and corruption flowed away from the bright lights of uptown and settled. Buildings were slated for demolition once upon a time but as the years passed and the economy tanked, the lower east side survived. Only the dregs live here. The whores, the low life hoods and people who have no other place to go occupy the old, rat and roach infested dwellings.

Bars line the main street along with hookers who for a fiver will rock your world and then knock you in the head and take the rest of what you've got. The cops patrol here, but only on certain days of the week, then they just breeze through, sometimes stopping and talking to the girls, maybe even getting a free roll in the sheets if one of the girls feels like it. Keeps the cops happy and they're pimps out of jail.

I live here. Have lived here since the darkness took over and snuffed out the light. I mind my own business most of the time, usually warm a seat in Kelly's bar where the strippers shake and shimmy their thick thighs to the beat of rock, blues or some other music played on the theater sound system, the damned thing costing more than the bar was worth. Some of the other bars have some lookers who dance on the stage but Kelly doesn't pay much and only the older gals and sometimes a semi-looker graces the spotlight.

Still he draws a pretty good crowd. Most of the patrons regulars who come here to drink until they puke and then drink some more. I come here because my apartment is above all this muck, the beat of the sound system that plays the strippers songs vibrates the floor and makes it hard to get any sleep. So I come down here, sit at a table in the back corner, nurse a glass of Jack Daniels and watch the crowd.

I was at this table the night she walked in. A tall blonde, her skirt hugged her hips like a second skin and the sweater she had on did the same. The gal was well built, as my friend Jimmy would say, 'built like a brick shit house'. She was halfway over to me when one of the guys at the bar spun around and stood up in front of her, weaved a little from too much hooch and grabbed her arm.

The music was too loud for me to hear what he said to her but she stepped up close, a big grin on his face that turned into a mask of pain, her stiletto-shod foot came up and then down, the spike slammed down hard on his instep and pierced the leather top of his shoe then jerked free. His scream was louder than the music and Ox, Kelly's bouncer showed him the alley.

She came on, her hand dipped into the little purse she carried and pulled out one of those long cigarettes ladies like her smoke, clipped it between her fingers and floated into the chair across from me, the cigarette finding purchase between her lips as she leaned toward me for a light. I picked up my Zippo and struck flame, the light giving me a look at the face of a goddess.

Her blond hair was cut to frame her face which was slightly long but not enough to mar her beauty. She had a petite nose that turned up a little on the end and a chin with a slight dimple in it. Her lips were full and red, the kind of lips that made a fellow want to grab her by the neck and kiss her hard until her lips hurt then do it again.

She drew deep on the cig, let some of it drift out then sucked it back in. She had deep blue eyes that were cold but hot. They drilled into me and made me sweat and chill at the same time. She leaned back and blew smoke, her voice like velvet when she spoke.

"I hear you're a man who will do just about anything for the right amount?"

I leaned forward on the table and drilled her back, my eyes and hers locked in a deadly embrace.

"Depends on what the job is and how much." I said this low but loud enough that she could hear. She smiled, pearly whites flashing back. What light there was in this joint reflected on them. The pause between us was a long one, then she gave me a throaty chuckle and flicked ash off the butt and leaned closer toward me.

"I want someone to take some pictures for me, pictures that will ensure my safety when I need it." She drew on the cigarette again, this time letting the smoke roll out of her mouth like dragon's breath as she waited for my reply.

"Pictures of who?" I asked and pulled a cigar out of my shirt pocket and clamped it between my teeth.

"An admirer is all you need to know. If you take the job I will pay you very well, in fact, there might be a bonus in it." Her leg found mine and traveled up, her shoe off as she worked her way onto the seat of my chair and onward. I smiled and grabbed her foot, slid it back to the edge of the chair and dropped it to the floor. A pout touched her lips and I laughed.

"How much," was all I said, my eyes back on hers, the pout disappearing.

"Five thousand. Half now and half when the job is done."

I leaned back, grinned and shook my head, no reaction from her face came back at me, her eyes still locked with mine.

"All or nothing," I said, "half and half don't work for me."

"How do I know you won't take the money then not do the job?"

"Baby, when I take a job I produce. I ain't no thief. Five G's up front or you can find another sucker to do your dirty work."

For a moment I thought she was gonna stand, flip me the bird and walk off, but she didn't. Her smile came back as her hand went in her purse and took out a roll of bills big enough to choke a mule on and tossed it on the table. Then the hand went back, this time produced a slip of paper and tossed it beside the bills. I leaned forward and grabbed up the bills, too many eyes had settled on the wad and I didn't want to have to kill anyone tonight over them. The paper was next. I opened it and read the address on it, The Carlton Hotel, right on the edge of Hell Town. A sleaze bucket of a place where the rooms could be rented by the night or the week, time and day were even written on it.

I folded it and slid it in my shirt pocket and nodded at her and then she stood like she was attached to wires it was so smooth, ground her cigarette out in the chipped ashtray on the table and kissed at me. I nodded at her and she headed toward the front door. Nobody spun and tried to stop her again. Nobody wanted a spike through their foot.

***

Sure, the job sounded like a blackmail racket. The pictures probably of some sugar daddy who was getting a little tight with his money and she wanted more. She did mention they were for safety reasons. Insurance to keep whoever the sugar daddy was in place. Either way I needed the money. Mason riding me to pay my tab and my bookie threatened to break an arm if I didn't pay him. I could do that and more with the five bills I had.

And if you need to know, yes, I am a PI but only in title. My license and hardware permit are still in effect but just barely, and I'm not an honest one like you read about in the paperbacks. A buck is a buck and since my rep had been scuttled I take jobs where I can get them. Don't get me wrong, I still have a sense of right and wrong and if a job sounds like it is gonna be wrong I tell the asker to take a hike. I have too many enemies in the can to end up there. I don't have a regular office though so I keep my PI equipment in Kelly's office, bottom file drawer cabinet. I knocked and then walked in, Kelly behind his desk with a little chippie on his lap, both of them giggling and snuggling up to each other. I think I'm gonna be sick.

"Somethin' on your mind Stoner?" His voice was raspy and the girl giggled.

"Yeah, first, I came to pay you what I owe you and second I came to get my camera and last but not least, how old is the sprite sittin' on your lap?"

Kelly cussed, grabbed the bills out of my hand and told me to mind my own business. She was old enough and that's all I needed to know. I got my camera and checked the lens, the cap still in place and a little dust had collected on the body since I last used it, probably more than a year ago. I grinned a nasty grin and spun, hit the shutter and the flash went off. Kelly jumped to his feet, the girl slid onto the floor, her butt slapped the wood and she squealed.

"You son of a bitch!" Kelly yelled at me. I laughed, flipped open the back of the camera and showed him it was empty then headed for the door. Closed it just as an empty beer bottle smashed against it. I headed upstairs to see if I had any film left or if I needed to buy some before all the festivities plus clean the dust off of it. I paid good money for this baby back when I was doing good business, back before the dustup that caused a young girl to be killed. I don't like to think about that part of my life too much. I have dreams still yet. Bad dreams that wake me sweating and screaming into the night.

I cleaned the camera, couldn't find any film, which I would get tomorrow so I sat down at the table that was piled with empty bottles and past due notices. I hunted around until I found one half full and poured me a glass, downed it and poured again. Maybe tonight I would sleep better if I could get plastered. Then again, maybe not. I'd lived in this hole for the last four years, my rep being tarnished by the shooting that I couldn't stop.

She was sixteen and the guy who had her was a bad ass, off in his head and killed for the fun of it. I'd cornered him in and old abandoned store building where he had killed two other girls, butchered them right under the nose of this spotless city. I burst in on him just as he was about to brand her, the hot iron so close to her skin that it was blistering her. I fired, the .45 slug caught him in the hand and knocked the hot iron out of it. But he was fast and felt no pain, just rage that I had stopped him from having his fun. He pulled a .357 from the back of his pants and aimed it at her head, his eyes wild and his laughter loud and insane.

Before I could fire again he blew her head off, the report usually the last sound echoing in my mind when I wake up from my nightmares, her head dropping forward and then looking up at me, her eyes asking why. I did what he did to her only more so, his head a red mush after I emptied my clip into him. If I had of been a hair quicker…

Of course I took the fall for her death. I should have called it in. Should have waited for the police to get there. Yeah, like they would have made supersonic tracks to get there before the girl was tortured out of her mind. They let me keep my license and pistol permit but the newspapers splashed my picture all over the front page, 'rogue PI causes girl's death'. I was cooked and made my way down here. Here they didn't care whether I was right or wrong.

Here they only cared about themselves and didn't give a damn about my misery. But I was still a PI, still a gumshoe and they respected me. Well, some of them did.

Around two I stumbled back down to the bar, paid for a full bottle of Jack and started to go back upstairs when Max grabbed my shoulder and stopped me. Max is an independent, you need a man to take care of a problem which involves cracking heads he's your guy.

"That dame that was in here, she hire you for a job?" He had a cigarette in his mouth and it bobbed up and down when he spoke, looked like one of those pencils you held at the end and shook it, the barrel looked as if it was rolling in waves.

"Yeah, paid me five grand to take some pictures." I leaned back against the bar. "Why?"

"No reason, she just looked familiar. When you supposed to do it?"

"Tomorrow night. There something I need to know Max?" I leaned back and he grabbed me before I fell to the floor.

"No, just I've seen her somewhere. Hell, enjoy it while you can buddy." I slapped him on the shoulder and smiled. I turned and made the stairs, staggered up the steps then crawled into the bottle and passed out. I didn't dream at all.

***

I woke around noon, the sun blazing through my window and when I opened my eyes it felt as if old Sol's rays were trying to laser my eyes out. I groaned, turned on my side and tossed my arm out, said arm landed on something besides the other side of the bed. I opened my eyes and stared. Something was under the sheets. Dark spots stained the whites and the smell of coppery blood tickled my nose. I jumped up, staggered back a bit, leaned forward and tossed the sheet back. The blond dame was under the sheets, her eyes stared at the ceiling and a second smile, cut almost to the bone, looked back at me.

My head felt like a concrete block and I thought it was pounding but then I realized it wasn't my head that boomed, it was someone at the door.

"Stoner, goddamn it Stoner open the door!" It was Max's voice, muted but thundering on the other side. I grabbed the door and tossed it open just as Max was about to hammer another ham sized fist on it. He started in, froze in the doorway and his eyes went wide and a 'holy shit' came out of his mouth.

In three steps he was over to the bed looking the dame over, not touching anything with his hands but doing it with his eyes. I groaned as he turned toward me, another two steps and he grabbed me by the arm, his voice low.

"Get dressed shamus and do it quick." He walked over to the bed, started to pick up my shirt and saw it was covered in red. A muttered damn it came from between clenched teeth and he turned toward me.

"Get another shirt and get dressed. The cops are hauling ass here so move it!"

I did, the mention of cops made my head clear and my feet move. While I dressed, Max and another guy I'd seen in the bar wrapped the blonde up in the bloody sheet, tying it off and rolled her into another one. This one they tied off too and then they hauled her out of the room. Kelly came in after them with a mop and bucket to scrub the floor. Why? I couldn't tell you. With all the new forensic techniques they have nowadays, they can gather a pinpoint of blood from the floor. Max came back in after a few minutes and grabbed my arm, hustled me to the back stairs and down them. Once outside he took me around to where a car waited, a brunette behind the wheel with a serious look on her face.

"Keep him out of sight Dot," he told her. "I'll get word to you when it's safe."

She nodded and started the car, pulled down the back alley and onto the street, driving slow and telling me to duck when a couple of police cars screamed by. We stopped close to the river, an old apartment building that looked like it was about to collapse appeared in my laser burned eyes. She parked around back, hauled me out and up the back stairs into the place, the back hall we went down cluttered with bags of trash that the rats were working in. I kicked a couple and she told me to knock it off, someone might hear the noise, look out and that would be it.

There was an old elevator on the first floor, a dinosaur with a wire door and corrugated steel floor. She shoved me in, shut the door and hit the switch, the old gal shuddered and then started up, still shaking as we crawled up to the second floor. Once there she opened the wire door and told me to come on, she wasn't gonna carry me. I stumbled out and followed her, her room on the back by the fire escape.

Inside I collapsed in a big chair, the cushion and back so soft I thought I would sink to the floor in it. She started to raise the blinds and then thought better of it, not because it might make me moan she said, but because the building next door had a window in it. The old coot who lived there always peeked in when she was home she told me later. I closed my eyes and commanded my head to stop booming, the drum in it so loud it made my eardrums hurt. There was a nudge at my knee and I opened my eyes, Dot stood there with a glass in her hand.

She was a looker, more than a looker, she was damned beautiful. She wore tight jeans that hugged her legs like a second skin, the curve of her thighs slipped into a slim waist then curved out into a rack that strained against her blouse, the middle button looked as if it might go at any time. She had beautiful eyes, soft and sensuous and blue as the summer skies. She leaned down and handed me the glass, her girls loose under the blouse and jiggling.

"Drink up." She straightened back up. "It will stop the thumping in your head."

I nodded. Not a good thing to do. It hurt like hell to even move. I drank, the liquid a white color, gritty to the taste and feeling like sand when I swallowed. There was a slightly bitter taste to it and I made a face. She smiled, her full red lips parting slightly and showing pearly whites behind them.

"The white stuff is Bro-Mo, the bitter taste is my momma's cure for a hangover. Now drink up, all of it."

I drank it down, grit and all and she took the glass from me, set it on the table beside the chair and grabbed my arms.

"Now, you need to stretch out on the couch. Momma's cure will make you sleepy and take away the hangover."

She pulled me up, my legs helped some but when I got to my feet I weaved and she grabbed me around the middle. Her perfume filled my nostrils and her breasts pressed against me, full and firm as she helped me over to the couch and lowered me onto it. I guess I tried to pull her down with me and she laughed, took my arms from around her and tossed my feet up on the couch, my eyes heavy and the room faded for a second. Her smile appeared again and then the lights went out.

* * *

The slap across my face brought me awake quick. My eyes snapped open and another one followed it, this one harder than the first. I focused as another one was coming and my fist shot up and knocked the ugly bastard who slapped me off the couch and onto his ass on the floor. He cussed and jumped up, his hand drawn back in a fist, cocked and ready to fire. He never did. My other fist caught him between the legs and he screamed, dropped to his knees and fell to the floor in a fetal position. I sat up and was about to put a number nine in his face when I heard the click of the hammer of a pistol. I turned my head and saw them.

There were three of them standing behind Dot, her face black and blue, one eye swelled almost shut, her blouse ripped open and her jeans gone, what was left of them in a heap on the floor beside the chair. I stood, my head clear and my hands clenched in tight fists, the man in the middle behind her holding my .45 in his fist, the muzzle pointed at her head.

"Easy Stoner. I understand this piece of yours has a hair trigger and I wouldn't want this pretty little thing to be dead because you made a bad choice."

Councilman Bill Conner smiled but the smile had no humor in it. It was cold as was his eyes, hard and cold as a frozen lake in the winter. He nodded at the two men and they came over to where I stood. The guy with the soprano voice stood and groaned and moved back as the two stepped up beside me, one on either side of me.

"Now, I want to ask you some questions Stoner and think hard before you answer them like a smartass because each time you do, I'm going to use the sight on the muzzle of your gun to cut her pretty face up. A sight leaves some nasty scars which don't heal properly." He smiled his cold smile and the two goons grabbed my arms, both of them smelled of Vitalis hair oil. Hell, I didn't know they even sold the shit still yet.

"First question." His smile slipped a little. "The woman who hired you, what did she tell you?"

"She told me she wanted me to take some pictures."

"Did she tell you of who?"

"No, but that's kind of obvious now isn't it?"

He raised the muzzle of my pistol then lowered it and chuckled.

"Yes, I guess it is," he said. "I'll give you that one. She tell you anything else?"

"Just that they were for her safety."

"I see, well, I guess she wasn't lying." He laughed then, a loud baying laugh that would have made a mule proud. I shook my head and looked at the guy to my right. He shrugged and nodded back to Conner. The man had turned toward me, my .45 leveled at me.

"You should have told her no Stoner. Of course I suspected she was up to something and had her followed. When I heard she had hired you I figured she had told you what that something was, not to just take pictures to blackmail me with. You see, the Feds are checking out some discrepancies about me. Some associates of mine are under scrutiny over some of the construction jobs here in town. She knew about this because I trusted her to keep her mouth shut. Never trust a dame Stoner. They'll screw you in more ways than one."

I grinned. I knew what he was talking about, the woman comment and the Feds. The rumor was some of the jobs had been awarded to a fellow by the name of Aldo, chief hood here in the city. Seems one of those jobs ran into a little trouble, a whole wall, brand new, had collapsed and killed a fellow plus injured two more. It was investigated and the investigation led to the construction company owned by a company that was nothing but a name on paper. A front. That front had Conner's name all over it. Old Aldo is a smart guy don't you think?

"She was gonna squeal on me Stoner, tell the Feds all about my business dealings with Aldo unless I accommodated her with more money. I told her she had better think about it and sent a couple of Aldo's boys to convince her she wasn't doing the right thing. She 'took a powder' as you private dicks are so fond of saying and I finally caught up with her, convinced her to meet me so we could come to some agreement. While we talked I had her number traced and found out where she was. Women can be so ignorant sometimes, don't you agree?"

I grunted and glared at him.

"Well, I sent some of Aldo's boys over to settle accounts and she wasn't there, I suspected she had gone to hire you so they waited for her to come back. We had quite an interesting talk we did. She begged for me to not kill her and I didn't, the man standing on your right did, slit her throat from ear to ear then we wrapped her up and hauled her to your place where you were drunk and passed out. All that was left to do was haul her up to your room. One of the bar's patrons let us in the back for a twenty. He doesn't like you very much and we placed her beside you."

"Wait a minute." I arched an eyebrow at him. "If you killed her someplace else, how come there was so much blood? She would have bled out on the way there. The hotel I was to take the pics at is on the edge of Hell Town."

"Very simple, think blood bank plus some payoffs to a couple of cops made to frame you for her murder." He smiled again and he took a step toward me, the hoods tightened their grip on my arms. "Now, where would you like to be shot, in the head or the stomach? Mind you, a gut shot is a painful death."

"Neither." I tensed.

"Can't decide huh? Oh well…"

My .45 was coming up and I jerked back, the one closest to me catching the back of my head on his nose. He yelled and his hands loosened on my arm so I jerked it free and shoved him to the side, his hands held a leaking nose as he fell on the couch. The other hood I grabbed by the coat lapel, jerked him around in front of me just as my .45 coughed lead, his eyes going wide as I shoved him into Conner, both of them stumbled backward to the floor. The hood on the couch reached under his coat and I kicked out hard, my foot connected with his boys and he folded. I stooped and grabbed his piece from the floor where he had dropped it, a .38 but one can't be choosey, and I drilled him between the eyes.

Conner was pushing the dead hood off of him and was aiming at me, his gun hand free. I grinned and aimed, his eyes wide and he hesitated. I fired and he grunted, the .38 slug tore a hole in his shoulder and my piece dropped from his hand.

Suddenly there were arms trying to grab me. I had forgot about the fourth hood so I dropped and spun in a crouch and fired but mine wasn't the only shot that split the air. The roar of another .38 sounded from behind me, two slugs caught him, one in the chest, the other in his throat, he back peddled and fell to the floor, chocking out his last breath as I walked over and looked down at him.

***

Dot wanted to plug Conner until I convinced her he would be better off in the pen. She gave me the .38 she had hid in the side of the chair for just this purpose and then collapsed. I caught her and eased her into the big chair, Conner babbled all the while I did. Promised me the moon if I would just help him out. I grunted and went over to the phone, called the cop shop and told them to send some uniforms.

I walked back over to Conner, knelt beside him, a big old smile on my face as I ran my thumb over the sight of my .45. He was right, a muzzle sight can leave some nasty gashes when used properly and I knew just how to do it.